Women Come Alive!

Written

TO: Gwendolyn CRAVEN, thanks for your love for God & his Holy Word. I see you being blessed with a child being saved

By

Elijah L. Hill, Th.B, MBA

3/23/7

Women Come Alive!

Unless otherwise noted, Scripture quotations are taken from the King James Version of the Bible.

Published By Perfecting the Kingdom International in Arlington, Texas, April 20, 2005.
Book Cover Graphic Designer Anwar Gay
www.swamp_graphics@yahoo.com

Perfecting the Kingdom International Ministries
www.ptkim.org
Elijah L. Hill
P.O. Box 181937
Arlington, Texas 76096
hilsker@yahoo.com
For copies send an email to the above website, write the above mailing address, or call 214-636-7668.

Table of Contents

Dedication

The accomplishments of great women in religion are seen in the mothers, sisters, and wives that uphold the arms of men down through the annals of time, and who become the foundation of their successes. I take this opportunity to mention the first woman that I knew in my life that accomplished so many things for the sake of the Gospel of Jesus Christ. Mom, you were my inspiration to write books when I was a child, and I and my other sisters and brother put together your first book called, "A Nation Deceived," when I was only six years old. In the early sixties you opened up a mission for the homeless, where you brought in adults and children to teach them the word and feed them. You would acquire vacant lots from the city; we would plant food then give it away to those that were in need.

The mother of Moses was a woman of strategy and determination who would not accept that her son had to die. If she had not devised a way to save the life of her son, there would be no great man called Moses. Without Hannah, the mother of Samuel the Prophet, being the praying woman she was, Samuel would never had been born to anoint David King. Without Mary being an available and chaste vessel for God's use, Jesus would not have been able to pass through eternity with a prepared body, and fulfill what the prophets said, "A virgin shall conceive and bare a son….."

Thank you for being my mentor showing me the way to serve humanity and to let God be my final foundation when it is all said and done. It is with you in mind that I write and dedicate this book, "Women Come Alive," because it was listening to you praying and weeping in the night that motivated me to know God. Love, your Son, Elijah L. Hill.

Introduction

The rights of white women in American society were not even in existence, let alone the rights of a poor, female, African-American ex-slave. Yet, all of these influencing factors were superimposed upon Mother Lizzie Robinson's heroine accomplishments. Most females who tried to establish themselves as leaders within male dominated religious organizations did so to no avail. Many went outside the four walls of their traditional religious church congregations to organize women's groups, such as women's clubs and women's Christian councils, where female leadership was allowed. The women of America did not even receive "suffrage rights" until 1922. Mother Robinson established a precedence in 1911, 11 years before suffrage by exercising a level of female leadership unavailable to any female leader of her era.

The man who released Lizzie into her potential as a leader was none other than the Pentecostal pioneer, Bishop C.H. Mason of the Church of God In Christ. Mason observed the unusual phenomena that revealed itself at the Azusa Street Mission where black and white and male and female worked side by side to accomplish God's Kingdom work. Mason gave Lizzie the responsibility to organize female leadership within the confines of an organized denominational structure, a leadership opportunity unheard of for white or black females in her era.

By Julia McCord Omaha World-Herald Staff Writer Saturday September 21, 1991

The presiding bishop of the Church of God in Christ on Friday called on the church to go back to its roots in order to secure the future. At a press conference at the Red Lion Inn, the Rev. Louis H. Ford of Chicago said Omaha is a key player in the effort. "Omaha can do more to bring us back to where we want to go than any other city in America," Ford said. "That's because the (church's) roots are so deeply planted and woven together here." Omaha was home to Lizzie Robinson, who Ford said was one of the church's "pioneering ladies."

In 1911 Mrs. Robinson helped the denomination's founder, Bishop Charles H. Mason, organize and structure the church. She was the first supervisor of women's auxiliaries. From modest beginnings in Lexington, MS, the Church of God in Christ has grown to 3.7 million members in 52 countries. But it has forgotten its traditional constituency, the disenfranchised, Ford said. "What did our church specialize in back then? He asked. "Grass-roots people." The church preaches a mix of Pentecostalism and entrepreneurship, training its converts in the ways of business as well as in the ways of God.

"The Church of God in Christ has always been a church that believed in economic development," Ford said. "The church works from the top down (God) and from the bottom up (business). During the Great Depression, for example, the church taught people to farm, to sew, to run businesses. In Memphis, a black-owned bank financed farmers and other entrepreneurs when times got tough.

Today, Ford said the church needs "to be the example for returning back to the roots of the real black church of America that lives for the people, by the people." We're going to stop turning our heads on the dope addicts, the prostitutes, "he said. With a "little bit more love, a little bit more care." 90 percent can be brought to Christ, he said.

The church needs to open child care centers all across America, halfway houses and shelters in every large city, and "get boys and girls to (the farm) to make them see livestock, let them plant fruit trees, teach them to be builders." Let's open some stores, stop marching and put the money to working," he said. "That's what our church is all about.

In the spiritual arena, Ford said, the church also needs to get down to business. It needs to carry Jesus' message of salvation out into the streets. "We still believe in all-night prayer, fasting, praying, clapping our hands and stomping our feet and screaming, " he said. "We will not run from our responsibilities in the community."

Church of God in Christ, Inc.
World Headquarters
Memphis, Tennessee USA

Office of the Presiding Bishop

Proclamation

Whereas: Our Late Founder, Bishop Charles Harrison Mason, envisioned the magnitude of including the women of THE CHURCH OF GOD IN CHRIST, INC., that they were in need of organization and direction while the National Church was in its stage of infancy, and;

Whereas: Our Late Mother Lizzie Robinson was appointed as the First General Supervisor of Women of THE CHURCH OF GOD IN CHRIST by our Founder, Bishop Charles Harrison Mason, in and around 1911, and;

Whereas: Due to the rapid growth of the Church and Mother Robinson's God-given skills in organizing, she gave great direction and support to the National Women's Work, by creating auxiliaries such as the Bible Band, Sewing Circle, Home and Foreign Mission, Sunshine Band, Purity Class, State Mothers Unit, and Secretaries Unit. Also, she prayerfully selected and appointed a hose of choice women, many of whom were sent to different States in the United States to be helpers to the Overseers (Bishops) that were appointed by our Founding Father, and;

Whereas: Mother Robinson hailed from the great City of Omaha, Nebraska, and she resided there until the date she was promoted to glory in the month of December 1945 while attending the National Convocation in Memphis, Tennessee, and;

Be It Therefore Resolved:

Bishop Vernon Richardson has appointed a State Historian in the State of Nebraska in order to research and verify that which will enhance the history of the CHURCH OF GOD IN CHRIST in the State of Nebraska under the auspices of Elder Elijah Hill and by the will of the CHURCH OF GOD CHRIST there in Omaha, Nebraska;

Be It Finally Resolved:

That the eighth day of July in this year of our Lord, one thousand nine hundred and ninety-two be a DAY OF MEMORIAL to honor the life and work of Mother Lizzie Robinson, the First National Supervisor who has fallen asleep in Jesus.

Given under my hand and the Seal of the Presiding Bishop at the World Headquarters in the City of Memphis, Tennessee, and written this 27th day of March in the year of our Lord one thousand nine hundred and ninety two.

L. H. Ford

Presiding Bishop

Mother Lizzie Robinson

Chapter 1

The Formative Years of One of the Greatest Organizers among Christian Women

The Early Years

Lizzie Smith was born a slave on April 5, 1860, in Phillips County, Arkansas. She was born during a historical transitional period, five years before the Civil War, and spent most of her childhood during the Post-Civil War Era. Lizzie's proud parents were Noah and Melvina Smith.[4] Her mother, Melvina, gave birth to five children. The awful human causalities of the Civil War devastated this family, leaving Melvina with five children and left Melvina a widow with the sole responsibility of care for the children.

Melvina was hindered in acquiring the ability to read because of the dehumanizing rules of slavery for African-Americans. When the Emancipation Proclamation freed all of Melvina's children, she made sure they received the benefits of an education and sent them all to school. Lizzie caught on to reading early and even started reading the Bible at the age of eight years old. Melvina was so inspired by this she would call over her adult friends and have Lizzie read the Bible to them. Melvina, encouraged by Lizzie's knack for reading the Bible, made this a consistent ritual in their home; providing Bible reading by her daughter Lizzie for her friends that were denied this privilege when they were slaves.[5]

Only white people were allowed to learn to read and write; if a slave was found doing so, they were subject to death. These former slaves were amazed to see and hear the Bible read by an eight-year-old African-American child, and they faithfully attended these Bible reading sessions in the Smith's home. Lizzie's mother realized that Negroes needed to create any self-help opportunity possible; especially taking advantage of any reading and writing learning opportunities.

Little did Melvina realize that what she was nurturing and instilling in Lizzie as a child would contribute to her becoming one of the greatest female teachers and organizers of Bible groups in African-American religious history. One thing that was impressed upon Lizzie at an early age by her mother was that education, reading, writing, and using her talent and skills could assist her fellow former slaves in bettering their illiteracy plight that was forced on them by American society.

Lizzie's father, Noah Smith, sacrificed his life for the cause of freedom during the Civil War, so that his fellow Negro slaves could experience the reality of the full equitable rights expressed in The Constitution of the United States of America. For seven years, between the ages of eight to fifteen years old, Lizzie was given an opportunity to read the Bible to these former slaves who without a doubt stood in amazement at this child's reading ability. Melvina Smith

Ida Holt, Lizzie's only daughter, High School Graduation, 1893

continued these Bible reading sessions for her friends and neighbors all the way until she died in 1875.

Upon her mother's death, Lizzie became an orphan girl, left to make her own way in the world at the early age of fifteen years old; but she never forgot her mother's teaching. She had to face the day-to-day struggles of life, mostly working for others, washing clothes in washtubs for a living. In 1880, at the age of twenty years old, Lizzie was married to Mr. William Henry Holt, and gave birth to her only child, Ida Florence Holt in Arkansas on September 10, 1880. Soon after the birth of her daughter, Lizzie was converted to the Lord. In 1881, after the untimely death of Mr. Holt at the age of twenty-one, she was wedded to a Mr. Woods. Mr. Woods died also a year later leaving Lizzie a double widow.

Miss. J. P. Moore: Mother Robinson's Early Mentor

Joanna P. Moore was born on September 26, 1832 in Clarion, PA, and she departed this life in 1916.[1] She was a 19th Century female Paul in the sense that she sacrificed her life to make sure that the generation of African-Americans, spanning 1863-1910, was not refused the opportunity to read a Bible.

As a Christian, Joanna realized that the state of America was such that illiteracy was the law of slavery and Jim Crow, and she knew that this would greatly affect African-American's in limiting their knowledge of the Holy Scriptures.

God gave Joanna a mandate to take the word of God not only to white Americans, but also to those that were refused the opportunity.

She was employed by The Women's Baptist Home Mission Society, who supported her in a work that not many other white women missionaries were willing to put their life on the line for. Most of her contemporizes thought she was crazy to take a chance to teach the Bible when society could make her pay such a great price for her dedication and commitment to her faith in Christ.[2]

Nevertheless, her faith in God was the foundation of her passion to fulfill God's will so that the next African-American child would not be deprived from the knowledge of the scriptures because of the dehumanizing effects of slavery.

Joanna did not commit to this work because she felt sorry for the blacks, but she felt that they were just as much God's children as white Americans.

Joanna crisscrossed the United States, living with African-Americans, experiencing life as they did, but with the mission of getting a Bible in the hands of any of them that did not have access to it.

She impacted eight states while establishing her work, and later on she taught and mentored Lizzie Woods to do this same work. The things that she instituted as she established her work in the kingdom were Bible Bands, prayer bands, and training schools for mothers, parent's meetings, sunshine bands, developed an Annual Mother's Conference, developed Annual Parent Conferences and developed monthly Religious Women's Newspaper.

Here is a listing of the states where she established schools and training centers for African-American women and children.

1. Helena, Arkansas - 1863-1865
2. Lauderdale, Mississippi - 1868
3. Chicago, Illinois - 1872-1873
4. New Orleans, Louisiana - 1873-1886
5. Memphis, Tennessee - 1886-1887
6. Little Rock, Arkansas - 1891-1895
7. Nashville, Tennessee - 1895-1896

Below is a testimony shared in 1864 by Joanna, from one of the Negro slaves she worked with in the south, telling of his fear of reading his Bible:

> *He destroyed all but his Bible; that he hid in a hole in the ground under his cabin floor. I will tell you his story in his own words as near as I can remember. "This Bible I used to dig up and read at midnight when all were asleep, and sing in low tones some of the hymns that I could remember. After a while I became less afraid and would read it late in the evening. Once, near dark, I was sitting away back in my cabin, so interested in reading about the blessed Saviour that I did not hear the master till he stood right over me. 'Osborn,' said he, 'do you know how to read?' 'Yes,' I answered all in a tremble. 'Did you know it against my rules?' 'Yes, I did.' He then snatched the book, tore and threw it in the fire. That was like taking the very heart out of me. I expected the hundred lashes but I prayed and the master walked out of the cabin without another word. I said, "That is God who shut the lion's mouth; He is the same God to-day." I had been preaching to the slaves about Jesus and singing the hymns that I could remember. Several got religion and one of them was Stephen, the servant who waited on master. He had been with him many years, had nursed him when a child. About a year after the*

loss of my Bible this servant got sick and died. The master was mighty sorry. As he sat by the bedside when he was dying, Stephen said, 'Master, I have one request to make; will you grant it?' 'Yes, Stephen, anything you want I would do,' 'Well, after I am dead, please master, let Osborn bury me. Let him sing and pray at my grave.' This the master promised. The cart came and carried the coffin to the servant's graveyard. The master was there on horseback, the other friends standing around the grave. I prayed and repeated some verses about the resurrection and sang, lining out the hymn. When I came to the words, 'The tall, the wise, the reverent head must be as low as ours,' the master uttered a cry and fell from his horse. The servants carried him away. The next morning he sent for me. Now again I prayed to Daniel's God, for I feared master would stop my preaching. 'Osborn,' said he, 'you may teach your religion here on my place as much as you like and as you have time to preach, but do not go onto any other plantation, for it is against the law. And you must be as quiet as you can.' That is the way the Lord opened the Red Sea for me. I never got another Bible until the Yankees came. The first thing I said to them was, 'Give me a Bible'; and I got one. That was as great a joy to me as freedom."[3]

JOANNA P. MOORE IN 1867

In the years following the Civil War the women of almost every denomination in the southland began to read Miss Moore's Hope paper and to organize Bible Bands in their churches. The paper contained wonderful lessons that motivated women to desire to obtain a deeper walk with the Lord. The Hope paper encouraged women to not just join a church, but to seek God and to live a sanctified life before God. Miss Joanna P. Moore taught in Louisiana until some of the white people in that area felt she was in violation of Jim Crow laws for teaching among the Negroes. The heavy climate of Jim Crow increased to the point of threatening her; they pinned a picture of a little coffin and crossbones at her door. Following the threats, she was frightened and up-set at how seriously the community's plot had thickened. The death threats against her caused Miss Moore to take refuge further north, fleeing for her life and moving to Little Rock, Arkansas.

The persecution that Miss Moore experienced would prove to be divinely directed because it was in Little Rock that she met and mentored Lizzie Woods, giving her the foundational strategies in developing and organizing women's prayer groups and Bible studies. The meeting of these two personalities helped to shape the future of the role of women in religion in the Pentecostal experience. Miss Moore did not allow the threats of white American society to blot out what God had called her to do, so she opened a new school, in Little Rock. She gathered the Negro women and children, brought them to her school, and continued to inspire the Negro women through teaching and prayer to have a closer walk with God. [1]

Even though Miss Moore worked primarily with African-American women to encourage them to learn the Bible, she never taught them to over step their authority with their male religious leaders. Below is her response when the women were being questioned for learning the Bible by African-American preachers.

All these years I have warned our sisters not to run ahead of the men but to keep their God-given place as "helpers," thus avoiding any confusion with the church. I always said, "Sisters, if the pastor objects to any of your plans, be quiet. Be good at home, teach your children and your neighbors and wait till God opens the door of the church." It meant much for our work to have the pastor present to hear the reports of the sisters and the lessons that I taught. "That woman has a work to do in the Christian church no one will deny. All are willing that she work and work hard, but what shall she do? If we can know God's plan that should settle it; therefore 'to the law and to the testimony.' In Exodus 15:20, we find Miriam led the women in song as they praise God for his wonderful deliverance. Surely she has a right to sing. After the children of Israel entered Canaan Deborah was appointed as one of the Judges, seemingly with the same power to control as Gideon, Judges 4. "Passing on to the time of Josiah when he found the long lost Bible he goes to the prophetess, Huldah, and she tells him what to do, 2 Kings, 22d chapter. We mention this to show that she may be a leader and a teacher. Years after, we find Anna, the prophetess, side by side with old Simeon, rejoicing over the infant Savior, and she spake of him to all. Luke 2: 36-38. Passing the long list of devoted women who earnestly obeyed the Savior through his weary

Joanna P. Moore & African-American women, Little Rock, Arkansas, mailing out Hope papers, 1902

years of suffering, we come to the Acts of the Apostles, and find Peter quoting the words of Joel, 'I will pour out my spirit upon all flesh, and your sons and your daughters, there is neither male or female in Christ,' Gal. 3:28. In Acts 21, we are told that Philip had four daughters who prophesied. In Romans 16, Paul mentioned a long list of women who labored with him in the Gospel, and gives Phoebe a letter of introduction to the church sending her on a Christian mission, requesting the church to help her, not as they thought best, but as she "had need of them." Again we find John, the aged, dedicating an Epistle to the 'elect lady.[1]

Miss Moore's spiritual impact in the Arkansas area was mightily felt as she faithfully taught the Bible until many women and men turned to God around the year 1891. As the women read their Bibles, many began to organize Bible Bands in their own local churches and clubs. Many of the women used the Hope paper written by Miss Moore in order to set-up and organize their Bible Bands. This early movement among the Negro women created an opportunity for many to learn and develop their teaching and leadership skills with each other. God used this Bible Band and prayer meeting movement to raise-up Negro women who would go from house to house reading the lessons from the Hope and praying for more love.

Around the time that Lizzie moved to Pine Bluffs, Arkansas the influence of the Hope paper was mightily felt in the Baptist church. The Baptist congregation that Lizzie became a member of gave her first introduction to the Hope while she attended the Baptist church Bible Band. She received her first copy of Miss Moore paper. Reading the Hope it made her begin to hunger for a deeper religious life, and at the age of forty-one years old she sought to obtain the experience of sanctification. Lizzie realized that she had a deep spiritual hunger that could not be filled by anything else but God and his work. Ironically, although Miss Moore had to flee to Arkansas, God had predestined Lizzie to meet and be tutored by this great white missionary. Miss Moore would be the mentor in the life of one of the greatest organizers of women ministry in African-American history. Both Miss Moore and Lizzie moved to Pine Bluff around the same time although it took a full ten years before they met. Lizzie is quoted as saying, "I received my first Hope paper in the Bible Band of that church. Her life touched mine." Lizzie was made a teacher in the Baptist Church were she was a member. Joanna foresaw that because of Lizzie's calling, she should not do traditional manual labor, but her destiny was to be in the ministry full-time laboring for God's Kingdom. God allowed her to see the greatness of Lizzie's purpose in life long before her national work had materialized. She realized God had chosen this former slave, who made her living cleaning and washing dirty clothes, for some purpose that was beyond even Lizzie's early awareness.

God would use this movement of the Bible Band and prayer meetings led by Miss Moore to raise-up Negro women who would go from house to house reading the lessons from the Hope. It was something about this Negro, former slave, which stood out from among the rest that Miss Moore was compelled to mentor Lizzie. The Lord had predestined for these two women to meet and touch one another's lives. Miss Moore allowed God to lead her to nurture and groom her underdeveloped pupil, a pupil that possessed so much future promise for God's Kingdom work. [1]

Miss J.P. Moore is a great historic example of a white individual that assisted and aided Negroes in the fight against the racism created by slavery, even to the point of putting their life on the line. All through African-American history, especially surrounding the Underground Railroad there have always existed white individuals that advocated the freedom of Negroes. There have always existed white individuals who truly believed that the equality stated in the Constitution pertained to all races in humanity.

Bishop Charles H. Mason

Chapter 2

Mother Lizzie Robinson Meets Her Barak—Bishop C. H. Mason.

Bishop C.H. Mason and the Holy Ghost

The next important figure in Lizzie Wood's divine destiny was Bishop C. H. Mason. At the beginning of the twentieth-century, in and around 1906, the Spirit of God was revealing the Pentecostal Movement. Out of the Azusa Street Revival came an important figure, Charles Harrison Mason.

His impact upon the organizational structure of many Pentecostal founders of all races was significant, especially during the ten years following the Azusa Revival. Lizzie Woods would eventually work under Mason's organization.

In 1907, in Memphis, TN, Mason founded the Churches of God in Christ denomination, which would become one of the largest African-American Pentecostal bodies in American History that evolved from the Azusa Street Revival. Mason would become the next step in giving Lizzie Woods a platform to fulfill just what Mrs. Moore saw in her future.

Early in their relationship Miss Moore realized that if Lizzie could excel, additional education would only enhance, strengthen and compliment her God-given skills and teaching ability. Lizzie was so used of the Lord that Miss Moore followed God's lead and began to seek for a way to further Lizzie's religious education. Miss Moore petitioned the white Baptist Missionary Society on Lizzie's behalf to send her to College for two years. The Baptist Missionary Society heeded Miss Moore's fervent request and they sent Lizzie to the Black Baptist Academy in Dermott, Arkansas. It was not long before Lizzie's public standing as a teacher became known to the point where she was promoted to be the matron of the Baptist Academy.

Bishop C.H. Mason, while scanning the different areas where his three year old church organization was in need of development, realized he needed a woman capable of organizing his national women's work. Bishop Mason heard of Lizzie Woods and it was arranged for them to meet at Dermott Baptist College. He explained to her about his vision and about the Holy Ghost indwelling with the evidence of speaking in tongues that he received at the revival on Azusa.

Here is Mason's actual testimony of receiving the infilling of the Holy Spirit at Azusa, he stated:

> *"The sound of a mighty wind was in me and my soul cried, Jesus, only, none like you. My soul cried and soon I began to die. It seemed that I heard the groaning of Christ on the cross dying for me. All of the work in me until I died out of the old man. The sound stopped for a little while. My soul cried, Oh, God, finish your work in me. Then the sound broke out in me again. Then I felt something raising me out of my seat without any effort of my own. I said, It may be imagination. I*

> *saw that I was rising. Then I gave up, for the Lord to have His way in me. So there came a wave of glory into me, and all of my being was filled with the glory of the Lord. Therefore, when He had gotten me straight on my feet there came a light, which enveloped my entire being above the brightness of the sun. When I opened my mouth to say glory, a flame touched my tongue, which ran down in me. My language changed and no word could I speak in my own tongue. Oh, I was filled with the glory of the Lord. My soul was then satisfied. I rejoiced in Jesus my Savior, who I love so dearly. And from that day until now there has been an overflowing joy of the glory of the Lord in my heart."* [5]

Bishop Mason shared about his former Baptist background, but also how he discovered that the promise of Jesus spoken of in Acts 1:4,5 which stated, "*And, being assembled together with them, commanded them that they should not depart from Jerusalem, but wait for the promise of the Father, which, saith he, ye have heard of me. For John truly baptized with water; but ye shall be baptized with the Holy Ghost not many days hence,"* what was soon to be known as the infilling of the Holy Ghost.

Mason shared his experience at the Azusa Street Revival how many races came from far and near waiting before God in prayer and fasting for the first-century New Testament experience of being filled with Holy Spirit. He shared with her how he was filled with the Spirit with the evidence of speaking in tongues. He shared with her that the current Baptist faith she was in did not believe that this God-given promise was for the present day Christian. Lizzie Woods, because of her great hunger to have all that God had for her in the scriptures, accepted his scriptural soundness and testimony of the reality of the first-century church and she received the Holy Ghost by the laying on of Bishop Mason's hands. [7]

The Baptist Academy did not accept the doctrinal belief in the baptism of the Holy Ghost as a present day God-given experience, so they excommunicated Lizzie Woods from the Academy for accepting her belief in the doctrine of Pentecost.

Bishop Mason and the Role of Women in Ministry

In November of 1911, six months following her initial meeting with Mason, while Lizzie Woods attended the fourth Annual Holy National Convocation, she was appointed by General Overseer Mason as the first National General Overseer of the Women's Work. Unlike most of his male religious contemporaries, Bishop Mason believed that women should be out front in leadership roles, cooperating alongside men in church work. In the beginnings of the Azusa Street Revival until 1920, women were very visible in ministry. But within the Pentecostal movement there eventually began to be a decline in the visibility of women. Before this time white and black women preached, were licensed, and founded and pastored churches. His vision was that women leaders would work alongside male leaders with the women governing, organizing and facilitating other female leadership roles. This was not Mason's initial Baptist doctrinal viewpoint, where men were the only ones to preach the gospel or take part in the founding of congregations.

There are two primary factors that influenced Mason's belief: one was the historic fact that in African culture the senior woman in the family was looked to for a strong leadership role. The second was that Mason witnessed at the Azusa Street revival the gender issue being washed away during the outpouring of the Holy Spirit. Within Mason's Pentecostal organization, the women functioned in leadership and preaching roles alongside their male counterparts, assisting the men in the work of God's Kingdom. The men within the organization may have wanted to see the women as only a teacher and not a preacher, but eventually the historical differentiation between the two evaporated.

This move established an important paradigm for women during this era. Many women in other traditional African-American religious organizations tried, at the beginning of the Twentieth-Century, to establish a more formal leadership role within their own denominations. Unfortunately, their attempts were to no avail when compared to Mason's internal women's ministry in the beginning of Twentieth-Century Pentecostal Movement.

In fact, Mason skillfully allowed this coexistence in ministry between men and women, but also maintained God's divine order of male headship as a check and balance system. Women in ministry respected their male overseers along with their female supervisors within the organization. The women of Mother Lizzie Robinson's women's ministry worked under the support mechanism of a Pentecostal denominational structure. This was the first time in history that this pivotal and unique occurrence appeared in religious history. These women essentially became God's leading ladies, the historical spiritual Deborah's that paved the way for establishing women's visibility within traditional denominational structures in the Pentecostal and broader Protestant religious communities.

Mason's organization was only three years old, but his new Pentecostal denomination lacked the same level of participation of women as he had observed at the Azusa Street Revival. He only had men up to this point, but his desire was to see the coexistence of sisters playing their part in the Body of Christ. Mason did not want to go into battle without a Deborah by his side, and he began to pray for God to send him such a Deborah. Mason sought God for a Judges four experience of being the first Barak, realizing early on the importance of the role of a woman judge within the Church of God in Christ camp.

This moment in history parallels the scripture in Judges 4:8, which says, "*And Barak said unto her, if thou wilt go with me, then I will go: but if thou wilt not go with me, then I will not go. And she said, I will surely go with thee notwithstanding the journey that thou takest shall not be for thine honour; for the Lord shall sell Sis e-re into the hand of a woman*". Bishop Mason's prayer was to go with a Deborah at his side that was able to teach, direct and organize another army of Azusa Street Praying Sisters who would be willing to join him in spiritual battle, willing to go to war on the battlefield for his Lord. Mason realized what his contemporaries among denominational leaders of his era did not realize that creating opportunities for women to work along side men would produce an explosion like that seen at the Azusa Street Mission.

God was the one who created the unusual atmosphere at the Azusa Street Mission. For example; Mason had been exposed to sisters like Lucy F. Farrow, who was the niece of the famous abolitionist-journalist Fredrick Douglas. Lucy was noted in the history of the Azusa Street Revival as a woman of prayer who had the New Testament Apostle Peter's gift of the laying on of hands where individuals would receive the Holy Ghost. Through her testimony there are testimonies of hundreds of important leaders of the Pentecostal movement who instantly received the Baptism of the Holy Ghost as Miss Farrow laid hands on them.[7] Many of these individuals were men that were hungry and sought for the First-Century Church Day of Pentecost experience. At that time it was acceptable for the woman to act as spiritual midwifes assisting in birthing forth God's divine oracles into the earth. Many of these same male leaders later took a different position towards women in ministry, allowing the sexism of America to suppress the effects of women in ministry.

God did not ask the permission of the men when he, by divine providence, orchestrated how His Azusa would take place in America. Mason refused to go the same direction as others concerning their views on women in ministry, and with his Pentecostal denominational leaders he hungered and longed for the God-given effect of sisters walking along side the brothers in building God's Kingdom. Mason prayerfully sought the Lord about what role the sisters surrounding him would play in the work of God's Vineyard. He studied the scriptures, prayed and fasted sincerely about the matter. Finally, he concluded that he was building his movement without one of the most vital components, and could not go further without placing a Deborah in place within his organization.

The Lord said in Genesis 3:15, that He would bruise the head of the serpent with the help and assistance of a woman. All through the Holy Scriptures God has always had a strategic woman in place to consummate his divine plans. At Azusa, Mason saw the same divine cord of truth, and decided that if God needed a woman for his plans and purposes then he, similar to Barak in the book of Judges, also needed a woman. Why in the Azusa Street Revival did God place white and black women strategically in position to take the lead in distributing the message of Pentecost throughout the United States?

God, in all his wisdom, knew that women would faithfully carry the baby to term, and that she could be a midwife with a spiritual womb to promote a duplication of the first-Century New Testament Church experience. God realized that if you wanted to promote something, tell it to a woman and she will spread the news all around. Mason understood what Jesus was doing after his resurrection when he first met Mary Magdalene alone at the tomb. In John 20:17,18, it states, "*but go to my brethren, and say unto them Mary Magdalene came and told the disciples that she had seen the Lord, and that he had spoken these things unto her.*"

The first publishing of the gospel started with a woman. God wanted to entrust the initial message to a spiritual midwife who was pregnant with opportunity to push out the baby when it was time. It was time now for Jesus to open the eyes of the men to the fact that not everything comes from them. God uses women even to tell them things that are divinely appointed by God to get the work of His Kingdom accomplished. Mason realized that if his father in heaven used the women strategically in the Kingdom, he would not be left out. The importance of the issues that arose from this paradigm shift parallel similar relevant issues of today:

1. Lizzie being first called overseer by Bishop Mason is similar to our modern issue of women being called elders by men.

2. Bishop Mason was a male religious leader that fully supported and nurtured Lizzie's leadership role within his organization. This relates to today's issue where some women feel that there is not a good man that will stand firmly behind a good woman in ministry.
3. Women have always played a significant place in the success of men's' visions. As Lizzie did for Bishop Mason's organization, this set a foundation of successful female leaders who impacted twentieth-century Religion, setting records that had never been done before.
4. A woman, having a healthy relationship with a male who totally supports her ministry; Lizzie and Mason exemplified this standard for modern-day religion to follow.

Within his organization's religious corporate culture, Bishop Mason lifted the glass ceiling by allowing extraordinary leadership development opportunities for women.

Aimee Semple-McPherson

Pioneering Pentecostal Women

Many women today feel that historically the women in the Churches of God in Christ were not free in ministry. If you compare other women in traditional denominations you find that other Pentecostal organizations mainly recognized and licensed women only as "Evangelist". Pastors in congregations from most Pentecostal denominations would only allow women to come and minister as an evangelist, to be a blessing to their churches, but would not recognize them within their organization in a leadership capacity. There were isolated cases where white and black women were ordained as evangelists in the early days of the movement, but in most cases recognition from those organizations came as a result of those females establishing their own successful churches and ministries.

Most women, whether white or black, functioned independently of the more formal denominations that evolved from the Twentieth-Century Pentecostal Movement. There were many unsung white and black female heroines who played significant roles in the early spread of Twentieth-Century Pentecostalism, and without their contributions the movement could not have advanced so aggressively throughout the globe. One of the most prominent white female Pentecostals birthed out of the movement was Lizzie Robinson's contemporary, Aimee Semple-McPherson.

McPherson was the founder of the International Church of the Foursquare Gospel, and in 1923 built the five-thousand plus-seat auditorium called Angelus Temple, in Los Angeles, California. At this time she was first female Pentecostal leader to build such a magnificent and elaborate

Kathryn Kuhlman

facility for the work of God's Kingdom. Some of Aimee Semple McPherson's male contemporaries within the Pentecostal movement had not achieved as much within their own ministries. She was a trial blazer and a pioneering white woman who stood out amongst men and women, white or black, in Pentecostal history.

Later in the Pentecostal movement God raised up another great woman, Katheryn Kuhlman, who became nationally known in the 50's, 60's and 70's. During her time, she became the worlds most widely known female televangelist. Male Pentecostal leaders of all races fought many of the female ministries that evolved from modern-day Pentecost. This was not to say that all men functioned this way. Those that supported the women did so because God always has a remnant to fulfill his divine purpose. The difference between Lizzie's experience and that of Aimee Semple McPherson and Katheryn Kuhlman was that they did not have a Barak that would support them from an organizational and leadership perspective. [8]

In the cases of McPherson and Kuhlman they had to move outside of Pentecostal denominational lines in order to fulfill God's Kingdom work in their lives. They did not have the support of the white Pentecostal denominations to embrace them and their visions, similar to the support that was given to many men's visions. The Assembly of God went as far as acknowledging them as Evangelists, but did not embrace their overall ministry visions. They had to walk alone down a lonely path, being deprived of their own brothers' support. Nevertheless, their examples within history only expose the fact that if you do not have all the tools you need, drive and keep going forward. God will

Mother Robinson & Bishop C.H. Mason 1932

always have a ram in the bush. Aimee and Katheryn received a majority of their support from other men of other denominations who observed them as a unique God-given gift to the world. [8]

Even as Jesus was despised and rejected of men that would not esteem him, this did not mean that God did not call the vessel into position to fulfill his divine will and purpose. Therefore they were acquainted with a sorrow and grief that could not be explained in their lifetime, but they realized that all things work together for the good for those that love God. This does show us that as great as their ministries were, if God wants something to happen, there is nothing on earth that can stop it. It may be delayed but it will not be denied. Even as Christ endured the Cross for us, everyone has a cross to bear where you have to be willing to forsake all others in order to be married to the kingdom vision of the Lamb.

God called other men outside of their denominations to be their Baraks that held up their arms in the midst of the battle. The lack of support they received from the denominational structures was not an excuse to be bitter with men. They had only become like spiritual Josephs, treading the winepress alone, forging out a spiritual inheritance that only complimented the great archives of Pentecostal history in America. When scholars speak of the great exploits of those who introduced the Pentecostal experience, these two women can not go unnamed or unmentioned, because God held their hands down the lonely road of ministry to give them an expected end.

Missionaries, Evangelists and State Supervisors

Only within Mason's organization was this paradigm of female leadership recognized. Even though women were not ordained as pastors or elders, Bishop Mason allowed female leadership and leadership development within his organization that did not exist within most Pentecostal organizations. Within Mason's organization, women were ordained as missionaries, evangelists, and state supervisors of women. This opened the door for leadership development to exist in a way that was not allowed or acceptable within traditional organized religion in America. For over seventy years from 1911-80's these Pentecostal leading ladies were pioneers before any traditional African-American denominations allowed women to work in leadership and preaching roles. They essentially followed in the footsteps of Mother Robinson. They were noted revivalists, missionaries, evangelists, and founders of congregations.

With her organizational expertise, Lizzie created a national platform within Mason's organization that allowed the roles of prominent female leaders to become the leading ladies of the Twentieth-Century Pentecostal movement. These were the only Pentecostal ladies that had the support of a more formal denominational environment. This female army was recruited as missionaries, evangelists and state supervisors who took the front-line, forging progressive moves of God. This contributed to Mason's organization becoming one of the fasting growing Protestant denominations of the Twentieth-Century.

Mason's organization, in addition to great female support, had dynamic male evangelists and pastors that ministered and gave the foundation needed for the extraordinary growth of the denomination. In essence, women played a substantive role in bringing souls into the kingdom with the spirit of cooperation with male overseers: bishops, pastors and preachers. The women would start prayer and fasting meetings within new cities, and this created a platform that founded thousands of small flourishing congregations throughout the United States. This also created a need for Mason to appoint more overseers where newly formed congregations began to sprout-up in almost every state in the United States by 1925. The terminology used by mothers and missionaries for founding congregations was called "praying-out" or "digging-out" churches. After the state supervisor, evangelist or missionary would organize and pray out a group within a city then they would seek for one of the male ministers within the organization to be appointed as the pastor.

Mother Robinson, through the Prayer and Bible Band auxiliary, complimented and nurtured a spiritual environment similar to that of those individuals seeking God in the Azusa Street Revival. Bishop Mason and Mother Robinson realized that prayer was the foundation upon which the New Testament apostles and the Azusa Street Revival were established. Mason knew that to establish a continual Azusa Street environment he had to encourage Lizzie to organize these Prayer and Bible Bands throughout his system of local churches. Matthew 21:13 states, "*And Jesus said unto them, it is written, My house shall be called the house of prayer; but ye have made it a den of thieves.*"

Mason recognized the vital importance of prayer to keep the lifeblood of his organization flowing. He greatly desired to maintain the essence of his Azusa Street experience, and to duplicate a prayerful church that society would have to recognize was a peculiar people and a symbol of a house of prayer. The spiritual base of New Testament ministry is to birth out of prayer, fasting, and waiting for God's sanctioning of the assembly. Acts 1:14 says, "*These all continued with one accord in prayer and supplication*". As an Apostle of the Azusa Street movement he wanted to share his earlier experience of the essence and necessity of prayer as a foundational tool of his organization. Mason had experienced his initial Baptism in the Holy Spirit at the Azusa Street Revival in 1906, and as he lay before God his hunger for God caused him to experience, like Jacob did, that certain place.

In Genesis 28:11, 12 it says, "*And he lighted upon a certain place, and tarried there all night, because the sun was set; and he took of the stones of that place, and put them for his pillows, and lay down in that place to sleep. And he dreamed, and behold a ladder set up on the earth, and the top of it reached to heaven: and behold the angels of God ascending and descending on it.*" Genesis 28 further states, "*And he was afraid, and said, How dreadful is this place! this is none other but the house of God, and this is the gate of heaven.*"

Mason knew, as Jacob did, that if Mother Robinson and the women of the church could recreate this certain place experience that took place at the Azusa Street Mission through all-night prayer and fasting meetings, his vision of sharing his Azusa experience of God's power would influence and impact his constituent's lives. He knew about the hunger for God that ignites with a sacrificial time of prayer and fasting that would manifest miracles, signs and wonders. No one could withstand being close to the fire of God's glory without his or her life being changed forever. Mason was not satisfied alone with new congregations established throughout the United States, but he wanted the people to know when they walked into his local churches that the gates of heaven had been opened, and the angels were ascending and descending. They would have to testify as Jacob had that this is the house of God, and that he abides in this certain place.

Therefore, in the early church it was a mandate to not just know religiosity but to know God personally and demonstrate ministry with signs following. Lizzie's first assignment was to establish houses of prayer by organizing local churchwomen into prayer warriors and intercessors for God. As Bishop Mason had wrestled with the angel that night in the Azusa Street Church in 1906 it was his deepest desire to have the flock that God made him national overseer of to become true God chasers. The unspoken understanding was that to be saved was to not just accept salvation and live right, but to demonstrate your faith with signs, miracles and healings following your walk with God.

Mason's Mission and Movement

Mason left his Azusa experience but refused to be denied the opportunity to contend for the faith that was once delivered to the saints at the Azusa Street Mission. Holding firm to the scripture in Jude 1:3, which states, "*Beloved, when I gave all diligence to write unto you of the common salvation, it was needful for me to write unto you, and exhort you that ye should earnestly contend for the faith which was once delivered unto the saints*," Mason's heart was not just to uphold the relevance of the importance of speaking in tongues as the initial evidence of the Holy Spirit Baptism; he desired not to change the setting that God had designed for its success and growth. Following are three fundamental principles in Mason's movement:

A Consecrated Life of Fasting and Prayer

A consecrated life of fasting and prayer was not an option: his church was prayed out with all-night shut-ins with fasting. As the old church mothers would say, if you don't fast you don't last, and if you don't pray, you won't stay.

Signs Following the Believer

Signs following your life were part of the common faith in the Twentieth-Century Pentecostal Movement emanating from the Azusa Street Revival. One of the common statements surrounding this point that later developed into a gospel song was, if you got good religion you ought to show some signs. In the scriptures, Mark 16:17, 18 states, "*And these signs shall follow them that believe; In my name shall they cast out devils; they shall speak with new tongues; They shall take up serpents; and if they drink any deadly thing, it shall not hurt them; they shall lay hands on the sick, and they shall recover.*" In early Pentecostal history there are many incidences when someone died and the church prayed until something happened, or they were raised from the dead.

A Commitment to Holy Living

One of Mason famous sayings from the scriptures that penetrated his denominational culture was found in Hebrews 12:14, "*Follow peace with all men, and holiness without no man shall see the Lord.*" The emphasis from the older saints was that you had to live right in order for your testimony to have any real substance.

The growth of Bishop Mason's movement centered on outreach, all night prayer meetings and evangelism led by church laity. People experienced in the local church that it was essential to their faith that laying before God carried an anointing with signs following: like healing, deliverance, miracles and people raised from the dead. Lizzie's assignment was to raise up an army of women intercessors to continue with the spiritual culture of the Azusa Street Revival.

Bishop Mason demonstrated to his men the example how prayer and fasting contributed to experiencing the miraculous ministry of the New Testament Apostles. Many of the men within his organization understood that you could not have a ministry without a dedicated life of prayer and fasting. Their own leader was partaker of the same discipline, and he walked it out before them with signs following. Mason's ministry was forged out of an intense dedication to God producing supernatural results like miracles, tumors drying up, the lame walking, the blind seeing, and even tornadoes and storms being controlled by his prayers.

From Bishop Mason's personal testimony of his healing ministry he states:

> *"Tumors have been removed from the bodies of women who have been suffering for years, only through faith in God. I met with an Elder who had hemorrhages of the lungs. He was a remarkable sight. The physicians said that it was impossible for him to live. God, through prayer, rebuked the bleeding, and today he is blessed of the Lord and is preaching the Gospel and saving souls. Bless His sweet name. Also through prayer of faith to the Lord, the lame have been able to put down their crutches and walk, and the blind*

have been made to see, the seemingly dead have been restored to activity again." [5]

Mason defined ministry as Paul the Apostle did not by titles or excellence of speech, as it states in 1 Corinthians 2:4, 5, "*And my speech and my preaching was not with enticing words of man's wisdom, but in demonstration of the Spirit and of power: That your faith should not stand in the wisdom of men, but in the power of God.*" The miracle ministry of Mason was an established precedent that inspired the male and female, white and black constituency of the organization to seek God's face to become true God chasers.

An eyewitness to Mason's anointed ministry was written by one of the leading ladies, Mother Dabney, who was appointed and trained, under Mother Lizzie Robinson tutelage. Her testimony states about Mason's anointed ministry:

> "*One day at Memphis, Tennessee during a large baptismal service, Bishop Mason was preaching on the banks of the river. A great windstorm arose, the multitude did not know what to do, but he lifted up his hands and face heavenward. As he prayed, the Lord gave peace. All was well. This event was so amazing, that it got media attention. News reporters wrote and published articles about it telling the city how God worked through a man who prayed.*
>
> *I shall never forget the time when a great tent meeting was in session in the city*

of Memphis. Fervent prayer was part of the great preparation for this soul-saving revival. Bishop Mason was led to spend many hours in prayer on the ground. Suddenly a terrible storm arose; it seemed as if the hour of destruction had come. The spirit of the Lord lifted him off his knees and he cried unto the Lord to send peace and rebuke the storm. The Lord answered him immediately.

One evening Elder RE Heart announced his text under that same tent. His subject: "Except ye abide in the ship you cannot be saved." Suddenly a tornado struck the tent. It was traveling so fast it seemed as if everybody was going to be hurled into judgment. Bishop Mason fell on his face and prayed. He arose and rebuked the devil, and God answered his prayer. After that the revival fires broke out and the Lord confirmed his word with signs."[9]

Mother Woods

Lizzie's first mission was to organize an army of women who complimented Bishop Mason's prayer and fasting mantle as warriors on the front-lines, carving out the astounding numbers of souls being swiped into God's Kingdom. Mother Woods was appointed in 1911 at the same time that thousands of white Pentecostals that came out of the Azusa Street Revival came into the Church of God in Christ under Mason's leadership. Noted scholars document this phenomenon from 1911- 1914, during which time Lizzie also assisted in encouraging prayer groups within the white

Church of God in Christ churches. Lizzie was called up to work with white females during a time when racial prejudice and Jim Crow was at its height.

The spiritual base of New Testament ministry is to birth out of prayer, fasting, and waiting for God's sanctioning of the assembly. This is what occurred with the Bible Bands and all-night prayer shut-ins that were essentially Azusa and First-Century church experience relived all over again; where congregations were founded by Mother Robinson's leading ladies. Lizzie appointed and sent out supervisors in every state to establish the local work while she continued to do the same nationally. In turn, these supervisors appointed missionaries or female evangelists to go out and save souls for God's Kingdom. This essentially brought forth a great harvest of souls, which added to the compliment of great preachers within Mason's movement.

The selection process for ministry development of the New Testament Church was birthed out of a fasting and prayer environment, as in Acts 13:2 "*as they ministered to the Lord and fasted, the Holy Ghost said, Separate me Barnabas and Saul for the work whereunto I have called them. And when they had fasted and prayed, and laid their hands on them, they sent them away*". The foundation for the birthing process has been laid already for the establishing of a great move of God, and the church today has to embrace their past to flow into their future. All of the individuals who came out of the Twentieth-Century Pentecostal movement, that have had great ministries today, can attest to having sought God in fasting and prayer for the anointing that causes others to look on them in amazement.

Most white women that evolved from the great Azusa Street Revival that were preachers of the Pentecostal faith had to function independently as evangelists and pastors as Pentecostalism moved toward a more traditional organizational structure. Even crossing traditional denominational lines, notable African-American ladies have tried to encourage male dominated leadership to allow an internal women's organization, but to no avail. Bishop C.H. Mason took an important position by implementing the phenomena that revealed itself at Azusa that male and female as well as people of all races worked together in cooperation. In 1911, Bishop Mason was the first apostle of his era that wanted to use the terminology of National Women's Overseer as the title for Mother Robinson. This title was consistent with the title of Bishop today. This caused such uproar within Mason's organization that he later changed the terminology to National Supervisor.

Even so, Mason maintained the essence of what God's power created surrounding race and women roles, despite his contemporaries who later formed more elaborate Pentecostal organizations but excluded this essence from their organizational visions. Not only did Mason set the standard for the future surrounding leadership development for women in ministry, but he also practiced interracial unity during the height of Jim Crow in the United States by ordaining thousands of white ministers. The Pentecostal Encyclopedia states, "*By ordaining ministers of all races, Mason performed an unusually important service to the early twentieth-century Pentecostal movement.*"

Mason appears to have been the only early Pentecostal convert who came from a legally incorporated church body, and who could thus ordain persons, whose status as clergymen was recognized by civil authorities. As a result, scores of white ministers sought ordination at the hands of Mason. Large numbers obtained credentials carrying the name COGIC. In the years 1909-14, there were as many white Churches of God in Christ as there were black, all carrying Mason's credentials and incorporation".[8]

In 1919, segregated practices emerged within Mason's organization, when the whites pulled away to form what is known today as the largest white Pentecostal organization in United States history, the Assemblies of God. Mason again became one of the most significant figures in modern-day Pentecostalism, by facilitating and acting as the spiritual father to the founders of the segregated white Assemblies of God organization. He truly embraced the essence of the Day of Pentecost that solidified itself in the Holy Scripture in Joel 2:28, 29, "*And it shall come to pass afterward, that I will pour out my spirit upon all flesh; and your sons and your daughters shall prophesy, your old men shall dream dreams, your young men shall see visions: And*

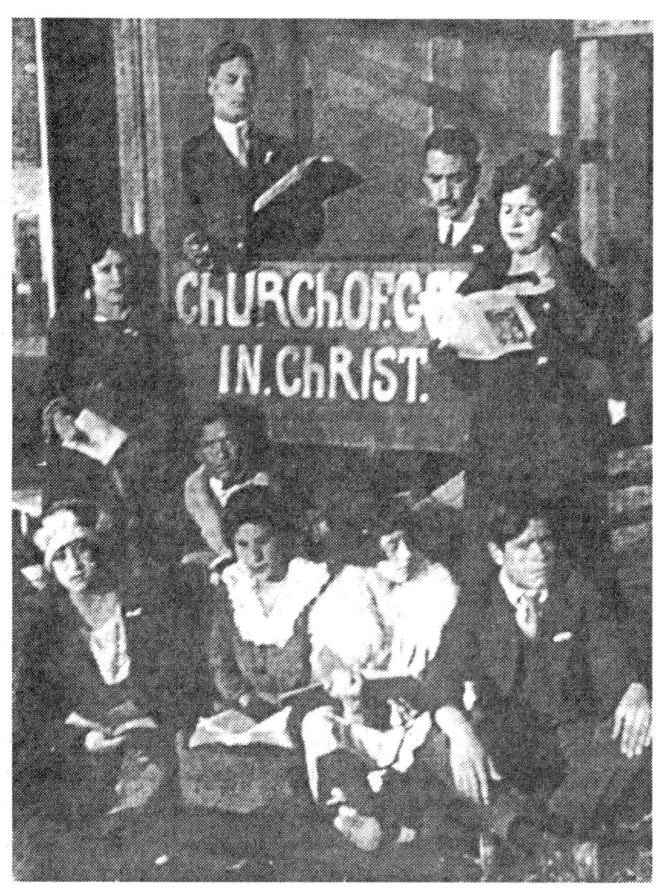

White Church of God in Christ Missouri 1917

also upon the servants and upon the handmaids in those days will I pour out my spirit."

Bishop Mason was also able to maintain his women's leadership development program within his organization. Despite male leader's opposition to Lizzie as a female leader, she retained the ability to appoint female leaders in every state in the United States. Bishop Mason was a strong believer in all the New Testament scriptures that supported his position that the call of God in leadership was not limited to men as spoken of in Galatians 3:28, which states, "*There is neither Jew nor Greek, there is neither bond nor free, there is neither male nor female: for ye are all one in Christ Jesus.*" Bishop Mason always maintained that everyone should have a covering and a spiritual head; therefore the women should be subject to her local male pastor and bishop. This rule of being subject to their spiritual covering did not just apply to females who ministered, but also to males in ministry.

On her first, tour in 1912, Lizzie states, "*I began then to organize the Bible Band in every local church of the Churches of God in Christ. She wrote, "It was my duty to have general supervision over all the women's work, and to appoint in every state supervisors to respectively do the same in their jurisdictions.*"[10] The work of the women had been started, but lacked organization. There were two groups that existed before 1911 that consisted of the Prayer Band and the Bible Band, which studied and taught the word among women. Mother Woods was inspired to rally these groups together based upon the scripture in Jeremiah 9 17-19, which states, "*Thus saith the LORD of hosts, Consider ye, and call for the mourning women, that they may come; and send for cunning women, that they may come: And let them make haste, and take up a wailing for us, that our eyes may run down with tears, and our eyelids gush out with waters. For a voice of wailing is heard out of Zion, How are we spoiled! We are greatly confounded, because we have forsaken the land, because our dwellings have cast us out."*[9]

Mother Woods also found a small group of women who were sewing called the Daughters of Zion. Mother Woods was inspired by scripture to encourage the sewing circle based off Acts 9 36-38 which states, "*Now there was at Joppa a certain disciple named Tabitha, which by interpretation is called Dorcas: this woman was full of good works and almsdeeds, which she did. And it came to pass in those days, that she was sick, and died: whom when they had washed, they laid her in an upper chamber. And forasmuch as Lydda was nigh to Joppa, and the disciples had heard that Peter was there, they sent unto him two men, desiring him that he would not delay to come to them.*"

In the beginning days of the women's movement, at the age of fifty-two, Mother Robinson traveled the first few years on foot from county line to county line in the Deep South. At that time, the organization was only in the states of Tennessee, Arkansas and Mississippi. Mother was so determined to organize the women's work that she walked on foot, setting up all-night prayer meetings, and developing Bible Bands in all of the first churches in the brotherhood. Later on, after raising initial finances for Mason's first national brick and mortar project in Memphis, she was provided with a horse and wagon to do her national travels to all the local churches.

The persecution was great in the early days of the movement. Mother Robinson would stand on the street corners and teach the word of God with power against lodges, and that people needed to receive the Baptism of the Holy Ghost. The experience of the Baptism in the Holy Ghost was looked upon from the traditional denominations as a new faith that was not biblical. Many crowds became violent towards her, and she had rotten eggs thrown at her while she taught and preached the Gospel of Jesus Christ.

Many early revivals had to take place in the back woods on farms. Many revivals were conducted in brush arbors, a distance away from the main town, so they would not hear the sound of celebration and praise to God.

At the age of fifty two to fifty six Lizzie experienced violent persecutions, like being thrown in jail and being beaten by crowds of racist and sexist individuals. These individuals felt that she had no right as a woman to be able to proclaim the work of God. Yet, she would not allow her suffering and persecutions to detour her vision for those women who would stand upon her shoulders. She realized that she was a trailblazer. She could not allow her sufferings of her present time to be worthy to be compared to the glory that was to be revealed. Her job, given to her by Bishop Mason, was to establish the women in the organization as prayer warriors and create a leadership development mechanism within the organization. She felt that if she had to die trying, then she would, but she would not give up knowing that God had called her into his vineyard to work.

Mother Wood's job was to organize and systematize the women's work nationally. Her first duty was to evangelize the national work. She then put together the Prayer Band and Bible Band into one unit and called them the Prayer and Bible Band. She also organized and encouraged the Women of Zion and called them the Sewing Circle. These were the first two auxiliaries established within the women's national work and to this day are recognized auxiliaries in every local church worldwide.

The other task that came to be a part of Lizzie's duty was to establish and help pray out local churches. The work was so new that working with new congregations and planting new churches became a part of her duties. Historically in the Church of God in Christ many of the earlier congregations were founded by a group of praying and fasting women that desired to see God move in their area. Once the prayer group began to grow to the point of forming into a possible congregation they would request a brother to come and take a lead role in organizing it into a formal congregation. Many of these prayer groups formed into what were later known as all-night shut-ins where individuals would learn to develop a closer relationship with God. The result was that many miraculous signs followed the intercessors that were birthed out of these small church movements.

Mother Woods used Jeremiah 9:17-20, as her scriptural foundation, which states:

> "*Thus saith the LORD of hosts, Consider ye, and call for the mourning women, that they may come; and send for cunning women, that they may come: And let them make haste, and take up a wailing for us, that our eyes may run down with tears, and our eyelids gush out with waters. For a voice of wailing is heard out of Zion, How are we spoiled! We are greatly confounded, because we have forsaken the land, because our dwellings have cast us out. Yet hear the word of the LORD, O ye women, and let your ear receive the word of his mouth, and teach*

your daughters wailing, and every one her neighbor lamentation." [9]

This essentially created a unique movement, which caused a greater outpouring of God's Spirit on the common people of the organization.

The Apostolic Work of Bishop Mason

Bishop Mason retained the true essence of being an apostle of the First-Century church by nurturing and encouraging the releasing of men and women's ministry gifts. He remained true to Christ, giving gifts to the church by allowing an environment where the saints were perfected for the work of the ministry. Bishop Mason's goal was to release the five-fold ministry into his newly formed organization. Today there are many individuals that are acknowledging the call to be an apostle in the Body of Christ. The only issue is that many carry the title, but do not understand the essence of the mantle of the Apostle. The First-Century apostle aided in the grooming and sending forth of other ministry gifts.

The Lord Jesus rose up twelve successors by spending time perfecting them for their future work of the ministry. He did not just build around himself; he wanted his work to live on beyond himself. Unfortunately, the focus of much of the Body of Christ today is to prepare servants for their own personal nations or kingdoms vs. being perfected as skilled laborers to win souls for God's Kingdom. The state of the Body of Christ is that they are too busy trying to serve God to the point where they do not take time out to commune with God.

We have replaced serving and becoming a worker with building an individual nation, and have left off our true purpose of bringing souls into God's Kingdom. In the local church, if people seek to go out in the vineyard to work, most leaders become afraid to allow their gifts to be sent forth so that God's Kingdom will come. Often the average Christian does not know how to lead a person to Christ; only ministers fill this role, and in some denominations the ministers do not know how to fulfill the great commission in their own neighborhoods. The everyday minister or Christian does not know how to be God's witnessing agent for the Lord of the Harvest.

Bishop C.H. Mason demonstrated the true essence of the first-century apostle mantle, and was the greatest example of an Apostle in the twentieth-century Pentecostal movement that personally received the baptism of the Holy Spirit at the Azusa Street Mission in 1906. His adamant desire to maintain the true essence of a first-century apostle allowed the type of growth that led to his organization becoming one of the largest African-American Pentecostal organizations in American history.

The purpose of a true apostle is to release and create an environment for other gifts like the prophet, pastor, evangelist and teacher to ignite and infuse growth into the Body of Christ. Bishop Mason was the person for this job since he had experience operating within all of the five-fold ministry gifts; therefore he had a heart to encourage apostles, prophets, pastors, evangelists and teachers. The women of the church played a vital role in founding congregations, and in the absence of a pastor would function in the teaching role and have acting charge of these newly starting congregations.

Mason's ministry also set the pace for filling auditoriums in national healing campaigns. He states from his personal testimony in 1916-1919:

> *"In the spring of 1916, I was invited by the authorities of the city of Nashville, TN to hold a camp meeting for the white people. The city auditorium, with a seating capacity of 7000, was furnished and equipped by the citizens of the city. One, Brother Martin, of the race paid all expenses of the auditorium. Many of the best white people of the city attended the meeting. The Holy Spirit through me did many wonderful things. On that occasion the rich and poor, wise and simple, were forced to confess that the hand of God worked in that meeting. I give the glory all to God. He is my strength. Another call for the whites, by CM Grace of Little Rock, Arkansas in 1919 in the tabernacle in Little Rock with a seating capacity of 7000 or more, God so wonderfully wrought His power among white and black, sanctifying, baptizing and healing."*[5]

Mason did not just wear the title of Apostle, but he did what the first-century church Apostles did: released other ministry gifts into God's Kingdom by giving them a platform to exercise their ministry. Today, within the Body of Christ, as we move closer to the return of Christ, there will be a need for preparation, mentoring and development of laborers so that they will become the nets to capture the great harvest of souls before the rapture of the Church. This is why Jesus saw the need to pray for laborers, that the harvest is plenteous but the laborers are few. Matthew 9:37, 38 confirms this when it states, "*Then saith he unto his disciples, The harvest truly is plenteous, but the laborers are few; Pray ye therefore the*

Lord of the harvest, that he will send forth laborers into his harvest".

Elder Edward D. Robinson - The Lapidoth

On her first tour, Mother Lizzie Woods met Elder Edward D. Robinson at the Gum St. COGIC in Little Rock, Arkansas; and they were married later that year. Lizzie Woods needed a unique man in her life, one that could support a woman in ministry and still feel secure within his maleness. Elder Robinson was just the right man at the right time. The famous saying is that behind *every good man is a good woman,* but that should go both ways: *behind every good woman is and can be a good man.* Elder Robinson gave her the liberty to organize the women's work of the Churches of God in Christ. He not only facilitated her rigorous travel schedule, but as a means to silence conflict traveled and evangelized alongside his spouse. Obviously this man believed in the ministry vision of his wife. [9]

Elder Edward D. Robinson, Lizzie's Husband

Chapter 3

Behind Every Good Woman Are a Few Good Men

The unusual relationship between Lizzie and her husband will go down in religious history. Unfortunately, this area of relationships tends to be a challenge to most individuals who do not find their unique God-given design in marriage. What was unique was that this relationship occurred during a time when women were generally mistreated by the sexist views in American society. Yet, the example that we see in scripture that parallels Edward and Lizzie Robinson's life is hidden in Judges 4:4, which says that Deborah was first a prophetess, second, the wife of Lapidoth, and third, she judged Israel at that time.

The good man within Deborah's personal life was her *husband Lapidoth.* Deborah needed a unique man in her life. What was the unique composition and dynamic that formed her ministry? What were the dynamics of Deborah's relationship with her spouse in order for her to fulfill her divine destiny on earth at her God-given time in history?

God gave this exact pattern to Mother Robinson for a husband. Elder Robinson was a Lapidoth. He assisted and supported his wife in her ministry next to Bishop C.H. Mason as the national mother of the Churches of God in Christ. Deborah was not only a judge, a public person, but she had a private life as a wife with a husband and family. Her example demonstrates that you can be effective in your private life and your spiritual destiny at the same time.

Sometimes we go to extremes of not knowing how to deal with the individuals God has given as our mates. Today you see people get married to individuals who are in ministry yet fight against them as they attempt to serve God. The reason this occurs is because two cannot walk together unless they be agreed. Just because an individual is a Christian does not necessarily mean they are committed and surrendered to God for kingdom work. When most people get married they marry for reasons other than what God originally intended. Mother Robinson was blessed to have a mate that understood that he would not place their relationship above God's work in the kingdom. Elder Robinson understood that his place was to assist her in the building of God's Kingdom, not to pull against her causing her to be ineffective for God. Genesis 2:18 states, "*And the Lord God said, It is not good that the man should be alone; I will make him an help meet for him.*"

Before you enter a marriage relationship you need to understand that you need to be content. One of the greatest mistakes made by Christians is that they want the mate so bad because of being lonely. They make the mistake of getting a man or woman that is a Christian, or non-Christian, but not sold out or supportive of God's Kingdom business. They look back later and say, well, I thought you were a Christian, but find that they worship the relationship over the fulfillment of godly purpose. They want you, not God. When you begin to spend time with God they feel you are betraying them for the Lord. Now, if you had waited on the Lord for the right mate, and understood that God is the one who will recognize that you are alone...!

When you recognize and remind God constantly that you are alone; this is an insult to him. Why? Because God knows what you have need of, and when God became interested in Adam's singleness Adam was not even thinking about the issue. God took it upon himself to consider Adam's singleness. When we are more concerned than God about our singleness then God will not give us our predestined mate. The Lord in His sovereignty wants to be the cupid and matchmaker in your life. When you take the throne and become the cupid is when even the most sincere people of God mess up their life. The Lord said he would make Adam a helpmeet for him. This means it would be someone comparable to him. Why is it that some of us married and our mate is not comparable to us in that they do not support us within God's Kingdom?

If you married them when you were saved, you did not wait on God. If you married them before you were saved then you just have to work with what God gave you, and let God walk you through the process. The Lord is the one who detected Adam's singleness, not Adam (see Genesis 2:18). The Lord is the one who brought the mate to Adam (see Genesis 2:22). If you are not married yet God is preparing you a comparable mate that is in agreement with your spiritual destiny and work in God's Kingdom. How can two walk together except they be agreed. God wants someone in your life that is in agreement with your love for God and love for working in His Kingdom. This was the scenario that occurred in the life of Mother Robinson. She was content to build God's Kingdom, and while doing so God gave her a mate that loved helping her, and was called to do that which God had called her to do.

C.H. Mason and the Marriage Test

It is a fact that some spouses try to hinder individuals in working within God's Kingdom. Many times the greatest fight lies within the private life of the individual in ministry. For example, C.H. Mason, one of the most important figures in Pentecostal history experienced one of his greatest tests within his first marriage. Mason fell in love with the beautiful Alice Saxton and allowed the relationship to distract him from ministry. Later, after their marriage, she emphatically told him that she was not in agreement with his ministerial plans for his life. She totally rejected him considering being in ministry. As God began to pull on Mason to begin to demonstrate his love for Him as the first and most important thing in his life, this created a problem for Alice, who divorced him for another man two years later. These circumstances in his life not only caused him to discontinue ministry for a period, but it brought him to the point of depression and contemplating suicide.[5]

In this example Alice looked like what Mason wanted, but she was not the comparable mate that God had intended for him. His comparable mate would have been in agreement with his purpose and spiritual destiny as Elder Robinson was for Mother Robinson. Mason was not content; he wanted the relationship so bad that he put off his ministry to achieve his goal. So many individuals in the Body of Christ go through this same process only to find out that God was not in the process. Many godly people even pray, thinking it is God, but are only overwhelmed by their own fleshly lust and desires. In his younger years Mason made a decision based upon the outward appearance, not knowing if the individual was committed to Christ and his call to ministry. Later, when Mason remarried, he realized that whomever he chose he must make sure she supported God's destiny for his future.

There is another scenario where God has shown you that someone is to be your mate. If because of impatience, fear of getting old, or seeing everyone else get married, you try to consummate that marriage before God has finished preparing that man or woman, it could become the worst experience for your life. It says in Genesis 2:18, 22, that God will CREATE a helpmeet for you; it was God who brought the woman to the man. God will bring the person to you; you do not have to go out to seek after the individual.

Look at one of the men who achieved one of the greatest ministries in Pentecostal history amongst African-Americans. He toiled with the same problems that most of us will have to go through or have already experienced. The Bible says that, *there is nothing new under the Sun.* This is why it is important to study the lives of those who have gone before; sometimes you can find a road map for your own life. Later Mason remarried, but by this next time he had learned a valuable lesson about marriage and relationships. The most important thing is that the person is a comparable person for you to fulfill your godly purpose in the earth vs. being an idol you have placed before God and His work.

This experience left an indelible mark on the life of Bishop C.H. Mason. It influenced his strong and adamant position in his biblical teaching that says; let every man have his own wife. His organization, at times, selected mates for individuals that could not discern who was the best mate for them. Many individuals in the early years of the church were told who to marry; making sure it was suggested to be someone strong in their Pentecostal faith. The older mothers were very adamant about not being unequally yoked with an unbeliever. Many of the old mothers knew the pain it would cause those that were new to the faith.

A teaching about double marriages within the Mason Pentecostal movement established a low tolerance for individuals marrying other people's spouses. In all cases the person in ministry who remarried while their spouse was still alive had to divorce and be reconciled back to their original spouse in order to be an active minister within Mason's early organization. If someone left their spouse to marry someone else, then they forfeited their credentials with the national church. They could no longer be a Minster or Pastor under the Mason movement. In the minutes of meeting in the early years of the national church in Memphis 1919, the elder's council would make reports on individuals that left their mates or took other men wives in marriage. They were removed from their position and not allowed to serve in the church.[11]

Marriage and ministry were held as the scripture had established: a most sacred institution that had to be honored and committed to at all costs except in the case of adultery. If ministers wanted to advance within the ranks of Mason's organization they had to be the husband of one wife, in other words not having been remarried while the original spouse was still alive. Mason went by the letter of the Holy Scripture, maintaining this foundation in the formative years of the church. I would even go far as to say that the Church of God in Christ has had a low divorce rate in the first seventy years of its existence, especially when ministers could not hold positions or advance within the denominational ranks without maintaining their marital status.

There are those within the Body of Christ that have not been brought up in a strict environment surrounding marriage, and they tend to be open to divorce for the wrong reasons. Others experienced marriage at a young age and become disappointed later when they were more influenced by what their flesh wanted rather than God's will. For example, some have experienced marital conflicts with individuals they were married to after they accepted the Pentecostal faith. Florence Crawford was a white woman who played a significant role at the Azusa Street Mission. She was the individual who maintained and published the mailing list for the magazine she published for the mission. When she accepted the faith of Pentecost and speaking in tongues, her husband of sixteen years rejected her as his wife.

The Word of God says that if the unbeliever leaves then the individual is not bound to them, so therefore they can remarry. Aimee Simple McPherson married a Pentecostal evangelist that came to her hometown. He died later while they were on a foreign missionary trip. She remarried another man two years later, tried to work out their marriage, but to no avail. She later divorced him in 1922.[8] This was one of the thorns in the flesh of Aimee Simple McPherson's ministry. She had a hard time getting her Lapidoth to line up with her ministry. Her husband was threatened as a man since she was the one God used the most in ministry.

Migration to Omaha

Lizzie's only child, Ida Woods, met her fiancé Archie Baker in Arkansas and they married and moved to Omaha,

Deacon Archie & Ida Baker

Nebraska.[9] Archie was drawn to the mid-western states, as many other southern African-Americans were, to find better job opportunities. Thousands of African-Americans in three great historical waves left the south around the beginning of the twentieth-century, when the American labor scene expanded from primarily an agricultural to an industrial base. The landscape of the south began to see major segments of its population exodus small farms to larger, more modern cities in the northern United States. Many individuals who left the south sent word back about factory work where you could be paid every two weeks instead of waiting all year for the result of a harvest.

Following their marriage, Archie and Ida Baker, heard about this northern and mid-western Promised Land, and decided to leave Arkansas and move to Omaha, Nebraska in 1912. The Omaha, Nebraska community in 1912 was experiencing extensive urbanization, and industrial prosperity and economic growth in the manufacturing industries which enticed many unskilled rural southern immigrants to move to the Omaha community. The Omaha community was flourishing with many industries that needed unskilled workers, for example packing plants, grain milling, lumber yards, furniture manufacturers, brick making, coal companies, petroleum storage and railroad companies. Many of these industries were established, since Omaha, Nebraska was right in the heart of the United States and the Union Pacific Rail Road would bring products in to be delivered to most of the Western United States. Omaha was a main transportation depot stop on the route across the middle United States. [25]

The North Omaha community, near 24th and Lake Streets, was the segregated part of town where blacks lived.

Mother Lizzie Robinson & Daughter, 1910

When Archie and Ida Baker moved to Omaha in 1912, the City of Omaha city directory listed Archie as working as a clerk at Frank Alley, living at the Oxford Hotel located at 306 S. 11th Street. In 1913, Archie is listed boarding with Gilbert D. Benson who resided at 2526 Ohio.[12] This same G.D. Benson later became one of the founding elders of another Church of God in Christ church years later, after becoming one of a first wave of new converts and coming under Elder Robinson's pastoral oversight for twenty or more years. Archie and Ida Baker roomed and boarded with several individuals from 1912-1921, when they began to rent what would become their first purchased home located at 2864 Corby in Omaha, Nebraska.[12]

By the end of her first year tour in 1913, Mother Robinson had established prayer and Bible reading groups with women within her organization. She concerned herself with improving the role of female ministry leaders that would work in alongside the male overseers that Bishop Mason appointed in each state. This opened a recruitment system that gave the women's department a national perspective. She traveled, constantly identifying the female capital that was lying dormant within the organization. As opportunities arose, she appointed supervisors to duplicate at the state level her vision nationally. She created an effective program nationally that was duplicated at the local level within the organization. Since women took to the front-lines with prayer and Bible groups, this created opportunities for a nucleus of new congregations to be planted and established all over the United States.

Lizzie framed an environment within a Pentecostal denominational structure that uplifted women into an important revolutionary autonomy that had not existed within the ranks of organized Protestant Religion. Mother

Robinson's leading ladies represented her throughout the United States; they duplicated her fervent vision for the women to be an army that would ultimately play a vital role within the growth and success of Mason's Pentecostal organization. Another very significant role that women played within African-American religious organizations was in their impact on fundraising within traditional churches. The financial strength and creative genius of women giving their support to men in ministry ensured success.

Fundraising and the National Headquarters Expansion

One of Mother Robinson's biggest contributions to Mason's ministry was her ability to raise money for his national vision; she would literally become the financial fuel within the organization's formative years. During a time when money was hard to come by, she developed a means of raising money through the organization's women's ministry. This set a standard for years to come that the women's ministry would become one of the biggest financial assets to the church. As her organizing of the women's organization expanded at the end of 1912, within one year she had raised $168.50 from the Bible Band she organized nationally. Through the virtues of consistent, itinerate travel Lizzie unveiled what was to become one of the best-kept secrets; the power of female capitol as an important financial asset to religious organizations.[10]

The value of the $168.50 Lizzie raised, at the turn of the twentieth-century, was a lot of money. The cost of living was ten times less than it is today. This amount was more closely valued at around a thousand dollars. When Lizzie

Mother Robinson 1912 during her first tour

finished her tour she gave this money to Bishop Mason and he was able to open one of two bank accounts for the national work. Here is Lizzie's personal testimony about her first year of work, "*Sisters, if you will, read your church paper about our organization. The Bible Band has been a great asset to the work. Brother Mason did not have a treasure in the work until we gave him from the Bible Band $168.50. We turned it over to Elder Mason, he put part of it in the White Banks and the other in the Negroes' Bank and said, Now, we went back the next year he had the Temple ready for us to have meetings.*"[10]

Bishop Mason used this money as leverage with the banks to undertake his first national headquarters expansion project. The national headquarters was located at 392 Wellington St. in Memphis, Tennessee, and the annual convocations had been held there for 4 years since their inception in 1907. Through the relationship established with the banks, the original building, a small frame structure, 40 by 75 feet, was rebuilt in 1913. This wooden structure was the first national temple. Bishop Mason commenced the reconstruction of this site as soon as he could, since the numbers of attendees to the annual convocation over the prior four years had outgrown the current building. They replaced the original building with a brick structure, 40 by 100 feet, with additional amenities added like a balcony, dining hall, kitchen, two rest rooms and a pastor's study.[13] This was the first expansion project undertaken by Bishop Mason, and Mother Robinson gave him the first financial seeds, setting the pace for aggressive brick and mortar projects in the national work and in other local cities.

Many of the organization's ministers who attended the annual Holy Convocation observed Mason's aggressive building programs throughout the years, and were encouraged to do the same in their home states. Bishop Mason's selection of Mother Robinson as a female national leader had proven fruitful and beneficial spiritually and financially to the work of the national ministry, and also encouraged other bishops in other states to see the importance of women in the kingdom, despite the initial opposition that flared up at the annual meeting a year earlier when Bishop Mason appointed her. Mother Robinson, with God confirming and sanctioning her appointment with divine results, the first year, solidified her future position within the church. She, with God's help, and her female constituency would for years become a secret financial powerhouse to under gird the national building programs. It was as if God in His divine providence had set the stage for this anointed woman of God to succeed.

Mother Robinson's experience confirms the eternal Word of God, which says in Proverbs 31:10, "*Who can find a virtuous woman? For her price is far above rubies*." This is a great example of what can happen when men and women work together in one accord, not fighting each other or one holding down the other. Lizzie had a good father in the gospel for her spiritual covering that believed in her work, and supported her even when other men within the organization had sexist views and wanted to hinder her ministry in God's Kingdom. To Mason's credit he established a historical standard by which all spiritual leaders can strive for; that is to be sensitive to the spiritual Deborah's that God raises up to be helpers in God's Kingdom. Leaders should understand that to use all of the spiritual resources that God has set before them in ministry would only be to their advantage. To not use women in ministry is like one burying some of the talents that could have brought souls into God's Kingdom.

Chapter 4

Mother Robinson Raises up an Army of Spiritual Deborah's.

E.M. Page and Mother Chandler

Edward and Lizzie Robinson continued to be evangelists, establishing churches in the western United States; and Lizzie continued to organize the women's work of the organization. Lizzie appointed about sixteen supervisors in the formative days of her administration to work alongside the state overseers to build up the local women's work.

Below are some of the first spiritual Deborah's appointed, listed by name and the state in which they organized the local women's ministry within Mason's Pentecostal movement:

1. Mother Bennie Roberts appointed over the women's work in the state of Arizona and New Mexico.
2. Mother Emma Cotton appointed over the women's work in the state of Southern California.
3. Mother Millie Crawford appointed over the women's work in the state of Southern California.
4. Mother Lizzie Robinson appointed over the women's work in the state of Arkansas and Oklahoma.
5. Mother Lula Williams appointed over the women's work in the state of Oklahoma.

6. Mother Jessie T. Simons appointed over the women's work in the state of New York.
7. Mother Lizzie Jones appointed over the women's work in the state of Colorado.
8. Mother Mary Little appointed over the women's work in the state of North Carolina.
9. Mother Jennie Watson appointed over the women's work in the state of Mississippi.
10. Mother Margana Kelly appointed over the women's work in the state of Georgia.
11. Mother Eliza Hollins appointed over the women's work in the state of Louisiana.
12. Mother Lillie Early appointed over the women work in the state of Kansas.
13. Mother Lucinda Bostic appointed over the women's work in the state of Illinois and Missouri.
14. Mother Catherine Hudson appointed over the women's work in the state of Tennessee.
15. Mother Hannah Chandler appointed over the women's work in the state of Texas. She was the first Supervisor to be appointed by Lizzie in November 1914.
16. Mother Rosa Vaughn appointed over the women's work in the state of Virginia.[7]

There were also several women evangelists that played a vital role in evangelizing the early church that worked under these state supervisors to bring many souls into the kingdom: Mother Cora Stevens, Mother Annie Driver, Mother Wyatt, Leatha Herndon, Ruth D. Herndon, Mary Renfro and Martha Renfro.[7]

Mother Robinson focused her first two years on establishing and organizing the Bible Band and the sewing circle. In November of 1914, she appointed the first local supervisor of women, Mother Hannah Chandler of Dallas, Texas to develop the women's ministry of Texas. At this time Elder E.M. Page was the overseer of Texas. Here is her personal testimony from 1925 surrounding her appointment, "*I was informed by the state overseer, Elder E.M. Page, that I had been appointed by Mother Robinson, Mother of the Women's Work of the state of Texas. When I read the letter, almost unnerved. I began praying the Lord to give me wisdom so that I might undertake, and when the Lord had given me wisdom how to take hold of the work I went into it with all my heart. At that time, there were only seven or eight churches, but today we have about 150. I have worked these eleven years with Elder Page and we have not had any trouble at all. We are glad to say that women's work is well organized in Texas.*"[11]

Mother Robinson knew this first opportunity would be an object of critical scrutiny for Overseer E.M. Page to demonstrate to the church that men and women working alongside each other would bring success to the national work. The ministry chemistry of these two, Overseer Page and Mother Chandler, witnessed

1st Woman Appointed as a State Supervisor, Mother Hannah Chandler, 1914

remarkable growth in the state of Texas. Overseer Page started off with an aggressive campaign to introduce the Pentecostal experience to Texas when he and mother started a revival in Denison, Texas where 100 new converts came to the faith. This resulted in the first church established there, with Page preaching his electrifying messages and Mother Chandler working the altar until the new converts experienced the distinctive evidence of speaking in tongues.

People were hungry with a deepening interest to know more about the New Testament experience, so Hannah taught them on the doctrine of Pentecost. Overseer Page developed a brilliant idea to host annual July convocations in different cities throughout the great state of Texas. The state of Texas was, outside of California, the largest state in the United States; and this traveling evangelistic type convocation and later a ministers and workers meeting helped to bring cohesiveness and growth to Texas in the early formative years. There were similar revivals conducted in Waco, Paris, Beaumont, and Hearne, Texas, and other cities where thousands of new converts all across the state of Texas dedicated themselves to the faith.

The fires of Pentecost through Overseer Page and Mother Chandler spread so far that it began to spread into the state of Oklahoma. They evangelized Oklahoma from 1916-1922, establishing churches and strengthening the faith in Muskogee, Kissentiner, Tulsa, Sand Springs, Shawnee and Oklahoma City, Oklahoma. Many churches were established and thousands of converts came to the faith. Pastors were appointed over these areas to serve the newly formed congregations. Many church edifices were constructed under the administration of E.M. Page[7]

Overseer E. M. Page of Texas, Appointed in 1913

within Texas and Oklahoma in the formative years of Mason's Pentecostal movement. Page was greatly influenced by Mason's aggressive building programs in Memphis at the world headquarters.

These early successes of Overseer Page and Mother Chandler had a very significant impact upon the church culture and foundational views of the importance of Mason's vision and divine guidance for organizational success. In essence, there were more churches established in Texas over a period of 10 years under Page and Chandler than all of the other states combined in the United States by 1925. Page was the consummate evangelist, as an overseer, because he turned his annual and semi-annual state meetings into evangelistic traveling crusades. His spirit and fervor for evangelizing his faith proved contagious. Many of his new converts, later called to the ministry, were so on fire for the Lord they began to spread the faith in other areas of Texas, and over the next ten years hundreds of new converts entered the faith and multiple congregations were established as a result.

Mother Chandler worked with all the new churches establishing Bible Bands and sewing circles amongst the women. The Bible Bands held true to conducting all-night prayer meetings to maintain the new convert's fire and power with God and man. The power of prayer and fasting behind their ministry created on-fire saints that spread the Pentecostal fire to many in their surrounding community. The Lord again placed his sanction upon the divine providential choice of this man and woman of God working as a team within God's vineyard. The woman's work continued with women digging out churches in areas of Texas where no pastor was established. The women working under Mother Chandler's supervision took on the frontlines in Texas, praying through new converts into the experience of speaking in tongues.

Mother Chandler appointed women evangelists and missionaries to validate their commission to work. Mother Hannah always worked with her overseer to get his approval on her selections and appointments. The ministry in Texas became so much for one woman as state mother; Mother Robinson stepped in to be the supervisor of Oklahoma.[7] The woman's work began to grow so fast she set-up an assistant state supervisor position for Oklahoma; the first time she set-up this office within the women's ministry of the church. Her national vision kept her constantly traveling, but in those states that expanded fast she would work until she found someone who could maintain the work within that state. In 1922, Bishop Mason appointed Page over the state of Oklahoma.

Digging Out the Church in Omaha

In 1915, the church experienced a great increase of female evangelists as many individuals received the New Testament experience with the evidence of speaking in tongues felt compelled to spread the message to family or relatives that lived in other parts of the United States. One pair of well-known female evangelists was the Renfro twin sisters (Mary and Martha). They had received the baptism of the Holy Ghost in San Diego, California in the summer of 1914, while staying with their father. They were so zealous for the Lord about having the baptism that they traveled back to their hometown in Moberly, Missouri in 1915. They began to spread the gospel in this community, and hundreds of new converts were saved and received the Holy Spirit.[7]

Chapter 5

From Arkansas to Omaha to Establish the Mother Church of Nebraska

The revival fires broke so much until word got back to overseer Barker, who later came down to assist them with preaching and teaching. The result was that a congregation was formed out of the initial evangelistic effort of these two young female, anointed vessels of God. At this time, in 1916, Mother Robinson wanted to relocate from the Arkansas Area to Omaha, Nebraska where her only daughter Ida Baker lived.[9] At that time no church was established for the Church of God in Christ in the Omaha, Nebraska area. Shortly after arriving in Omaha, Elder and Mother Robinson started making plans to dig out a church. The Lord directed them to pick an area in North Omaha, three blocks from the heart of the black entertainment center on 24th and Lake Street. This was a high traffic area as many people entered the Lake street area on their way to work or to transact business on 24th and Lake.[7]

They did not have a building, so they located a vacant lot near 27th and Lake Streets and began holding afternoon and night services. They took what God gave them to work with: their voices, their Bibles and their desire to see souls in the Omaha area come into the knowledge of the New Testament experience of being filled with the Holy Spirit.

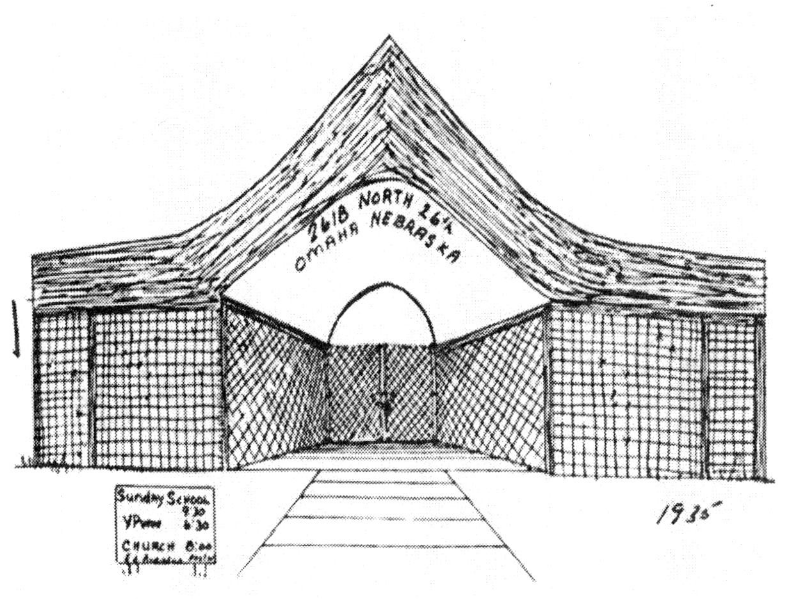

The Mother Church of Omaha, Nebraska, 1935

The Pentecostal message had not come to this area, so as crowds gathered around day after day to wittiness this man and woman of God expound on the scriptures, it seemed unusual to them that a female was just as adept at expounding the gospel as her husband, when this was not often seen in their traditional Protestant churches. The people could feel and observe that there was something different then what they had experienced at their churches. It made the crowds hungry for the new knowledge that was right in their Bibles all the time.

Their main message concerned the faith of holiness and that the baptism of the Holy Ghost was a present day experience for all believers. The crowds began to grow daily as people were attracted to this usual site taking place on 27th and Lake Street, and the word spread around about their preaching which caused many to be curious enough to come to see. Then many were convicted by the word of God to turn to God, or many turned to the faith of holiness desiring this closer experience with God that they heard about at the daily Lake Street services. As the crowds got bigger, many came to Christ, were healed and set free by the power of God, and soon they had to organize a church. The Lord had his hand upon the work as it began to grow rapidly, and the people were hungry to learn more and to develop a church family. The Robinson's church was the first Church of God in Christ Congregation in the state of Nebraska. Bishop Mason authorized his newly appointed overseer to Bishop V.M. Barker of Kansas City Missouri. He made a trip to Omaha, Nebraska to validate that the work had progressed and placed his approval on the local assemble.[7] Elder and Mother Robinson toured together for three years from 1912-1915. As the church kept flourishing and with increased numbers added to the church, Pastor Robinson finally had to stay home to feed the flock of God.

The history of the Nebraska church was closely tied to the state of Missouri's jurisdiction, since Bishop V.M. Barker was authorized by Bishop Mason to be its overseer in 1917. Bishop Barker became the tenth overseer of Bishop Mason's early state overseers. From this time on the Robinson's church would travel to Kansas City, Missouri for Bishop Barker's annual local convocations. Bishop Barker would play a very significant role as the local Bishop of the national supervisor of woman. Bishop Barker was a young man who had recently moved his family up to Missouri to establish a work in the Kansas and Missouri area. The Lord had placed a heavy anointing on his life, and he and his wife Ruth began in 1912 to pioneer this area for God's Kingdom. He not only was their local leader, but he played a vital role in spreading the Pentecostal faith all over the state of Missouri, establishing over 50 churches in the next 30 years. He became a very important personality in the Robinson's lives as time moved forward, so here are some additional insights on his background in the Mason Movement.

Bishop V. M. Barker

Virgil Moses Barker was born June 24, 1880 at Drew County, Arkansas. He was the son of William and Mary Barker. He grew up near Pine Bluff, Arkansas where he received his early education; he later attended and graduated from the Branch Normal, now Arkansas A&M College. While in school he visited his sister Amanda Stocker who won him to Christ. It was in her home that he experienced receiving the baptism of the Holy Ghost in 1907. Mr. Barker, being a young, single man taught school in Arkansas during this time until he felt God's call to the ministry at the age of twenty-seven years old.[14]

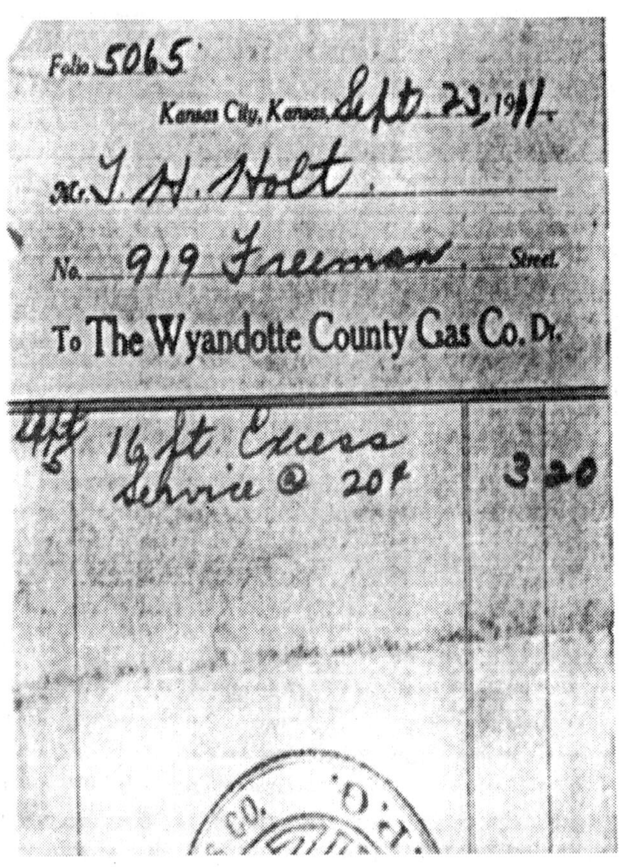

Folio 5065

Kansas City, Kansas, Sept. 23, 19[illegible]

Mr. T. H. Holt

No. 919 Freeman Street

To The Wyandotte County Gas Co. Dr.

4/15	16 ft. Excess Service @ 20¢	3.20

Elder Holt's Gas Bill when Elder Baker stayed in Kansas City, KS, 1915

He moved to St. Louis and while preaching at a church revival fell in love with a beautiful, already saved young girl named Miss Ruth Flernoy. They married in St. Louis, Missouri, June 16, 1910. In St. Louis Elder Barker began his first pastorate under Elder Williams, who had appointed him to his first charge, a small mission. He served as Pastor there until he heard the voice of the Lord commanding him to go into the entire world and preach the Gospel. He was stirred in his soul as he sought to obey his call. While prayerfully seeking the will of God as to where the Spirit would direct him, he was led of the Holy Spirit to come to Kansas City, Kansas and the Missouri area.

The following detailed information surrounding Elder Barker first coming to Kansas City, Kansas was conducted by two telephone interviews of granddaughters of the Holt family: Mother Evalon Jones (06/08/98, 05/13/98) and Mother Geneva Holt (06/17/98). Elder V.M. Barker, after a three-year ministry of being greatly used of God in St. Louis, Mo., was led of the Holy Spirit to move himself, wife and baby daughter Ruth to Kansas City, Kansas. He stayed in the home of the late early pioneers of Missouri, Thomas and Lucille Holt, who lived in Kansas City, Kansas. Elder Thomas Holt was ordained as an elder personally by Bishop C.H. Mason in Memphis, Tennessee on December 12, 1912. His actual license is signed with the personal signature of Bishop Mason.

The Wyandotte County Gas Company showed Thomas and Lucille's address to be located at 919 Freeman Street. Mother Virginia Lee, daughter of the late Bishop V.M.

Missionary Lucille Holt & Clifford Holt, 1922

Barker, states about her father in personal interviews on May 11, 1998 and December 30, 1998 that "*Papa was corresponding by letter with Elder Holt around the time the Lord was leading him out of St. Louis, Missouri. He wanted to establish a work on his own for God's kingdom, and Elder Holt shared with him how the Kansas and Missouri area would be an open field for new converts in the faith. So Papa, by invitation of Elder Holt came up a few months earlier than mother came.*" Shortly after arriving in Kansas, Elder Barker started with house services. As the Lord led him he preached holiness and eventually held tent services during the summer months. Many souls were saved, which developed into the first congregation in Mason's organization in the northern states of the United States.

Much persecution was suffered because of their belief in the Pentecostal doctrine; they were threatened, their services were ridiculed, scoffed and spurned, and their tent was burned to the ground. Yet, Elder Barker was illuminated even more to continue to preach because of the heavy anointing on his life. They did not have a permanent location so they went from house to house until souls were saved. Elder and Sister Barker yet filled with the enthusiasm and presence of the Holy Ghost established a mission in 1912 in Kansas City, Kansas at 3rd and Oakland. As was the tradition of the Mason movement Elder Barker took the new converts to the nearest lake and with the help of Elder Holt baptized them into God's Kingdom. In November 1912, with the help of God and an unmovable faith, Elder V.M. Barker traveled to the Holy Convocation in Memphis, Tenn., and represented this newly established seventeen-member church. [14]

A year later, after organizing this new congregation, Elder Barker appointed the late Bishop D.J Young to take

Elder V. M. Barker

In the year 1912, Rev. V. M. Barker, then an enthusiastic young man, full of religious zeal, came to Kansas City, Missouri, from St. Louis, Missouri, inspired of the Lord. He found a few loyal Evangelistic workers laboring there in an effort to establish a Church of God in Christ. Rev. Barker was accepted as pastor. A Mission was opened at Twenty-first and Flora avenue. People from all walks of life flocked to the standard of the gospel which he preached. The Church world was aroused, and members of this group became targets. The gospel preached was styled as a delusion operated by false ideas, hypnotic forces and practices, which caused many to leave their former faiths and creeds.

It was decided for the sake of those impressed, that something must be done to stem the tide of error.

The church labored on in the midst of many persecutions; a large tent was burned, and blackmail letters were written, ordering Rev. Barker to leave town under dire threats.

The church prospered nevertheless, and its progress was steady. Opposition diminished, and property was purchased upon which a church building was erected in the year 1916. The membership increased rapidly, among which were many young men who were called to the ministry of this faith. These young ministers having been qualified according to the requirements of the faith, were in turn ordained and sent into various sections of the city where they established churches, purchased properties and erected church edifices. Property valuation runs into the thousands of dollars.

Rev. Barker, as a result of his achievements, was appointed by Bishop C. H. Mason as Overseer of Western Missouri and Nebraska. His program for the future development of the church is in full accord with the system adopted at its General Meeting which convenes at Memphis, Tennessee, annually. His line up is as follows:

State Supervisor for Women.

Missionaries appointed to assist in the Evangelization of the State. Organization of Districts.

The appointment of District Leaders to assist in carrying on work in the territory of his jurisdiction.
Supervisor in her duties.

The appointment of District Missionaries to assist State

The raising of finance to help in the national efforts of the Church of God in Christ.

Rev. Barker has in his territory about forty churches and about fifty ordained and licensed ministers.

1st Revival Tract, in 1912, announcing Elder Barker on Flora Street in Kansas City, MO

charge of his newly developed pastorate. Bishop Young is significant because he was one of the original charter overseers that organized the Church of God in Christ along with Bishop Mason in 1907. Young and his family later became the national publishers of the Whole Truth News Paper and the Sunday school material for Mason's entire national church for fifty years. He was also one of the original of the two men that accompanied Mason to the Azusa Street Revival in 1906, where he and Mason received the initial experience of speaking in tongues. Elder Barker was not content to just pastor in Kansas, he felt led to cross over into the state of Missouri to establish God's Kingdom there also. He remembered what the Holy Spirit told him in St. Louis, Missouri, "To go into world and preach the gospel."

The Barkers, Holts and the Work in Kansas City

In the year of 1912, Elder and Mrs. Barker arrived in Kansas City, Missouri, full of fervor, enthusiasm, and religious zeal to help spread the Pentecostal message. Elder Thomas and Lucille Holt left Kansas following the ministry of Elder Barker into Missouri. Their spirits had bonded together like the biblical David and Jonathan, and they believed that Elder Barker would become a great builder of the Body of Christ. They had witnessed remarkable growth, and had seen how God's hand and anointing was using this young man. Elder Barker was bold as a lion in the face of opposition and with the strength of God's power he set his face as a flint in the midst of public persecution preaching the unadulterated word of God. He and his evangelistic team: his wife Ruth, Elder Holt and Sister Holt set out for Missouri. When he arrived he found these faithful women (Mother Early and her Sister Lillie, laboring there in an effort

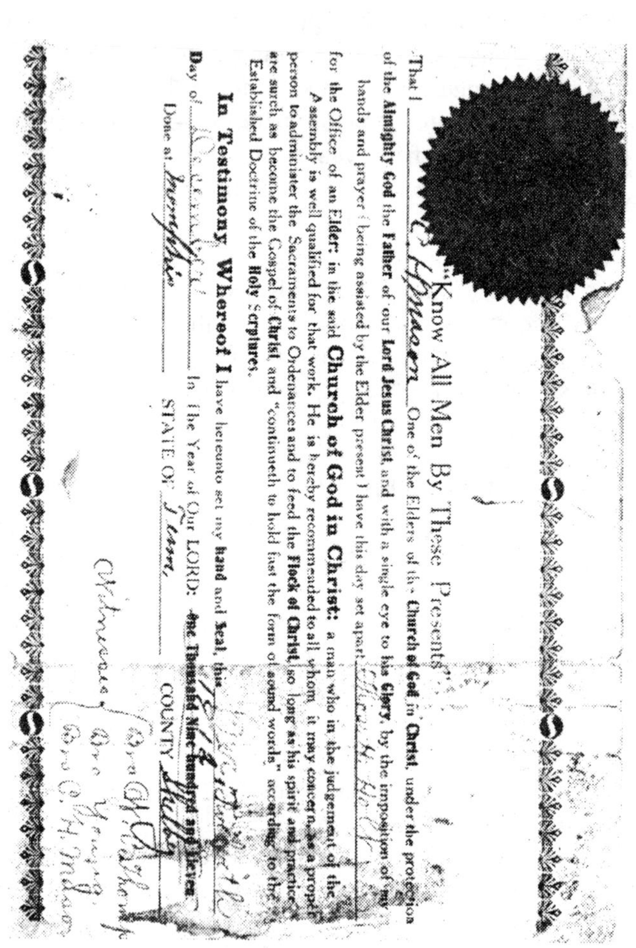

Know All Men By These Presents:

That I C. H. Mason One of the Elders of the Church of God in Christ, under the protection of the Almighty God the Father of our Lord Jesus Christ, and with a single eye to his Glory, by the imposition of my hands and prayer (being assisted by the Elder present) have this day set apart Thomas H. Holt for the Office of an Elder in the said Church of God in Christ: a man who in the judgement of the Assembly is well qualified for that work. He is hereby recommended to all whom it may concern as a proper person to administer the Sacraments to Ordenances and to feed the Flock of Christ, so long as his spirit and practice are surch as become the Gospel of Christ and "continueth to hold fast the form of sound words" according to the Established Doctrine of the Holy Scripture.

In Testimony Whereof I have hereunto set my hand and seal, this [illegible] Day of [illegible] In the Year of Our LORD: One Thousand Nine Hundred and Eleven

Done at Memphis STATE OF Tenn. COUNTY Shelby

Witnesses: [illegible]

Mason's ordination of Elder Thomas Holt, 1911

to establish a Church of God in Christ. He was accepted as pastor, then rented a small building on 21st and Flora, and began services. Soon a revival broke out as people from all walks of life flocked to the standard of the gospel that he preached. Many of the souls that were saved in Kansas City under his anointed preaching became important figures in Bishop Mason's cabinet in the early work of Mason's national organization, or they lived in the Midwest. For example:

1. C. G. Brown of Kansas City, Missouri, first executive secretary of the International Home and Foreign Mission
2. Anna Smith became general recording secretary, and personally dictated Bishop Mason's messages during the national convocations.
3. Bishop C. W. Williams became the International Sunday School Department Superintendent.
4. Mother Lizzie Robinson became the National Mother for The church.
5. Ida Baker, Lizzie's daughter, was treasurer of the International Home and Foreign Mission Department.
6. Bishop D. J. Young of Kansas City, Kansas became Publisher of the Whole Truth Magazine and of national Sunday school literature.
7. Bishop Charles Pleas, the first convert of Bishop C. H. Mason, later became Bishop of Kansas.
8. Dr. Arenia Mallory, who Bishop Mason met in Missouri, became the first female he appointed over his College in 1927.
9. Elder. F. C. Christmas, from St. Louis, Missouri, the first national Sunday School Superintendent for the church.

Bishop V. M. Barker Baptizing saints in Kansas City, MO, 1950's

Elder Barker labored on in the midst of many persecutions; members became targets, a large tent burned, and blackmail letters were written ordering Elder Barker to leave town under dire threats. The burning of a tent that he had set up for meetings frustrated Elder Barker's efforts. From the ashes of the tent, Elder Baker, accompanied by his wife, went to the streets and from house to house for ministry. Once, while out on the street, two white gentlemen approached Elder Barker. They mentioned that they understood that he had no place to worship. They invited him to look at a property on Highland Avenue, and arrangements were made to occupy this place. There were two houses on the property. Elder Barker used one for the church services and the other for a parsonage for his young family. It is at that same, divinely given, site, 1709 Highland, where Barker Temple was founded, December 16, 1916, where the Mother Church of Western Missouri now stands. [14]

Mother Virginia Lee, daughter of the Late Bishop V. M. Barker, stated in a personal interview on December 30, 1998, concerning the beginnings of Barker Temple, "*Some of the first charter members were Thomas and Lucille Holt, and Lucille Holt was one of the first deaconess appointed by Elder Barker. Elder Thomas Holt's son Clifford Holt was the first YPWW leader. Mother Gola Bell was also one of the first charter members at Barker Temple; she later started the Gola Bell prayer hour at 12:00 at the church. Sister Anna and her husband Clayton Smith attended the church. She would always find Papa's scriptures to read them aloud during his messages. Clayton and Anna Smith lived up on Paseo Street then, and when Bishop Mason came to town, he would stay with Anna and her husband. Anna Smith was also one of the first secretaries at the mother church for Overseer V.M. Barker in Kansas City, Missouri. She came to Christ through the preaching of Elder Barker at the 21st and Floral St.*

location where Elder Barker lived when he first left Kansas City; Kansas to start another work over in Missouri."

When I conducted a personal interview with Flernoy Barker, one of the late Bishop V. M. Barker's sons on May 11, 1998 and August 24, 1998 he assisted me in gathering information and identifying different pioneers of Barker Temple, who were the founding members of his father's early congregation from the early "20's-30's". Mother Beatrice Watkins, piano player at the time, and the oldest member of Barker Temple shared with me and assisted me in naming the early congregation of Baker Temple during interviews on May 11, 1998 and August 26, 1998. Some of the early pioneers at the inception of the Barker Temple, the Mother Church of the Midwest: Elder Virgil Moses Barker - Pastor, Sister Ruth Barker - Pastor's wife, Mother Early - first church mother, Sister Lillie, Elder Thomas Holt, Lucille Holt - first traveling evangelist missionary, Clifford Holt - first YPWW president for local church, Anna Smith - local church secretary, Clayton Smith, Bro. Harriston, Sister Pearl Harriston - Traveling companion who with Lucille Holt prayed out many churches in Missouri, C.G. Brown, Rosa Brown, Bro. Mitchell, Bro. Horn, Bro. Madison, Bro. Cooper, Elder Douglas, Clarence Williams, Ulysee Griddine, Esau Jackson, Elder Lockhart, Mother Picket, Sis. Gola Bell, Bro. Curry, Sis. Curry, Mother Fannie Jackson, Mother Crockett, Mother Nall, Brother Lee Nall, Elder Nance Rice, Bro. W.C. Thompson, Elder Goodin John Turner, Elder F.T. Taylor, Elder C. Range, Pauline Richards - first piano player for local church and Elder James Stewart - first Assistant Pastor to Bishop Barker.

The First Great World War

The Beginning of World War I for Americans was April 6, 1917. The institution of the draft laws, The Selective Service Act, had a major impact on American society. President Thomas Woodrow Wilson, the 28th president of the United States, at this time had just been re-elected for a second term in 1916. What was very ironic was he maintained a neutral policy about America entering WWI during his first term in office. The war had raged in Europe since 1914 without America's participation. Yet, Wilson's hand was forced when Germany began to attack American civilian ships. Even though he repeatedly tried to address it in a peaceful manner, the inevitable took place on April 6, 1917 when Wilson reluctantly requested The United States Congress for a declaration of war against Germany. There were hundreds of thousands of young men who were sent overseas to fight in this First World War. The death toll began to climb to the point where people began to feel the impact.

Bishop Mason delivered a sermon about the topic of WWI on June 23, 1918, a year or so after America entered the war. It took place in Memphis, Tennessee at one of his large baptismal services on the banks of the river. Elder W.B. Holt dictated his entire message. The title was "The Kaiser in light of the scriptures!"[5] Elder Holt was one of several white ministers who refused to depart from Bishop Mason's organization after most of the white Pentecostals separated from Mason to form what was to become the Assembly of God. Elder Holt, who was a former Nazarene, became the national recording secretary for Mason and as an attorney by trade was also a legal advisor to Mason. Elder Holt personally dictated this historic message surrounding WWI. In his message, Mason, "told the people to not look to the power of the United States, England, France or Germany, but trust in God." He was concerned with the war from the respect that God moved upon him to address the spiritual and scriptural meaning of this World War.

Eventually, that year, Bishop Mason had his attorneys to draft up a document stating his organization's stance on Christian's taking up arms, and joining the United States military on behalf of WWI. The stance that was written was to come to be known as the conscientious objector stance for the United States military. This position stated that it was against a Christian's religion to have to take up arms and shed another human being's blood for the purpose of war.[8]

This position had a great impact on people as many Christians wanted to refuse the draft, based upon their religious faith. Nationally, there were as many whites and blacks that followed the conscientious objector stance and other Holiness and Pentecostal organizations all over America agreed to this religious position. Because of Bishop Mason's stance, and his personal influence as a black man in Jim Crow times, where many whites were following an African-American's beliefs, many felt that Mason had too much power and influence over too many American Citizens, both white and black.

Some saw this as a threat to the American Government. The Federal Bureau of Investigation opened a file on Mason, and they tried to create a conspiracy that Mason's verbal statement about the government's war was treason against the United States. This action by the government created a very turbulent year, 1918, within Mason's organization.[8] Persecutions were unleashed as a windstorm of political power came to crush this young God-given movement by attacking the leader with false and frivolous conspiracies in an attempt to put him in prison for life. This was nothing short of attempting to break the momentum of the largest Pentecostal organization at the time. The ideology of white American leaders could not accept the fact that this religious movement that had so much impact on white and black Americans. With the founder being a member of the black race, they felt insulted that thousands of Americans would listen to Mason's voice over theirs. As Herod the King, who represented the government in Christ's day, wanted to destroy the plan of God to facilitate his own fleshly envy, so was it with the US government in 1918. Because of these attacks several things occurred in 1918:

1. Blytheville, Arkansas - Elder Payne tarred, feathered, and jailed for preaching on the conscientious objector stance from the pulpit.
2. Elder Mangrum of N.E. Michigan, the father of Supervisor Mary Johnson was fatally shot.
3. Mother Lizzie Robinson was jailed for spreading the gospel.
4. Bishop Mason had the FBI investigate him as a traitor of the U.S. government.
5. Bishop Mason was physically knocked down.
6. Mason was arrested in Lexington, Mississippi and placed in a county jail for several days.
7. Mason was barred by the Judge from entering the state of Mississippi for a year.
8. Mason was booked, and then transferred to federal prison in Jackson, Mississippi.
9. Mason was arrested in Paris, Texas then placed in jail again.
10. Mason was given trail dates for the district courts of Jackson, Mississippi and Paris, Texas.
11. The church had to come up with somewhere around $5000.00 to post bond during the different times

Mason was arrested and jailed in various states, in order to regain Mason's freedom prior to awaiting his trial.[5]

The dictionary of Pentecostal history stated through their research pulled from early FBI files in Washington:

"The impact of Mason's stance was so great on persons entering the military that the government tried in vain to build its own case against Mason for fraud and conspiracy. With other followers, Mason was subjected to a thorough and ongoing investigation by the Federal Bureau of Investigation, but all to no avail. When agents confiscated Mason's briefcase for what they knew would be incriminating evidence, they found only a bottle of anointing oil and a handkerchief with his Bible. The United States District Court in Jackson, Mississippi, failed to render a federal grand jury indictment against Mason and his followers. The "kangaroo court in Paris, Texas, in 1918, dropped its case when the presiding judge looked at Mason, laid down his books, and said, "You all may try him, I will not have anything to do with him." No courtroom, no government, no amount of persecution or prosecution could withstand the powerful witness of those pioneers whose lips had been touched by divine fire."[8]

Through this tumultuous season in the church, Mother Robinson continued her travels every year from state to state and church to church encouraging and strengthening the pastors at the local level. On many of these national tours, her daughter Ida Baker, who was a gifted singer, would cheer the hearts of the people. As Pastor Robinson could no longer travel with her, she chose some of the daughters in Christ she was mentoring as state mothers to travel with her to learn from her about the work of women's ministry. Some of the earlier women that accompanied her on her national tours were, Fannie Jackson, Lucinda Bostic, Jessie Strickland, Nancy Gamble, and Eliza Hollins. All of these individuals later were appointed as state mothers of other states and became noted revivalists, evangelists, and some prayed out congregations. [9]

The Sewing Circle

One of the areas of ministry she centered on after organizing the all night Prayer & Bible Bands was the Sewing Circles. The Sewing circle had a two-fold purpose: first, it was to show woman how to make clothing for their families, and second, to create a business out of their sewing talent to start an in-home business. Lizzie realized the importance of a creative woman was a financial asset to her home, and ultimately a blessing to her church and community. She established Sewing Circles in every church in the brotherhood, and she trained her daughters that were coming along to do the same.

The sewing circle was a beginning seed that introduced the importance of an entrepreneurial spirit with the women within the women's organization. This created a mindset for the women to not just be a good homemaker, but to have an economic impact upon their families, pulling themselves up from their bootstraps. Lizzie inspired the women to look to God for strength, which encouraged self-help. Mother Robinson realized that Christian women should embody the woman of Proverbs 30, who was industrious within her home, being prosperous with the works of her own hands. [15]

In Omaha, Nebraska the congregation continued to grow. Elder Robinson started looking for another property, which they purchased at 2318 N. 26th St. In the beginning, on this site; they held their services in an open field with a fence built all around it. Dad and Mother Robinson used to call this the tabernacle. This was their summer temple. To prepare the area they placed hay down on the dirt floors from the big barn that sat on the backside of the lot they had purchased. Several years later in the thirties they broke ground and excavated a cement basement where they held services. They built the structure according to plans, including in the basement bedrooms and a kitchen. Excitement filled the air when Pastor and Mother Robinson saw the vision begin to expand; because the new converts had a mind to work. As they raised sufficient money they completed the final phase of the construction, by completing the walls and roof of the upstairs sanctuary.

They made the final payment on the land contract to Mrs. Belle Miller for $2400.[16] They were giving the opportunity to raise the funds as the church grew, since the land contract allowed them the liberty to rent the land and later receive a quitclaim deed to own it. As they made the final payment toward their church land, the property transferred into the hands of the church. Dad and Mother Robinson were still living with her daughter Ida at her 2864 Corby Street address. They gave all of their money to support the vision of God's local assembly, just as most beginning church founders did that started churches from the ground up.

1st New Construction of Mother Church Pastored by Dad Robinson Omaha, Nebraska

Mt. Hope Cemetery

In the year of 1920, Dad and Mother Robinson decided to compliment the National Church's vision by purchasing, in the name of the mother church, a burial plot for their church members. It was purchased at the Mt. Hope cemetery. The entire early membership of the mother church is buried in Lots 83 and 84 on 75th & military in Omaha, Nebraska. Here is a list of the first burials and names of the early members of the mother church in Omaha, Nebraska. Finally, Dad and Mother Robinson were both buried on the same plot of land they had purchased for their members.

MT. HOPE CEMETARY COGIC LISTING LOT 83 & 84

1.	Arron Silwells	Oct 1, 1923
2.	Andrew Cheney	Jun 9, 1929
3.	Mary Mitchell	May 28, 1930
4.	Sultana Hawkins	Nov 22, 1930
5.	Vivian Nevills	May 23, 1931
6.	Jesse Green	Oct 1931
7.	Sally Kinsey	Nov 1931
8.	Richard Stewart	Jan 1932
9.	Nathan Frierson	May 1932
10.	Mollie Owens	Sept 1932
11.	Fannie Richman	Dec 1932
12.	Bettie Williams	Jan 6, 1934
13.	Edna Greigg	Mar 1934
14.	John Beefkin	Mar 1936
15.	Robert Wallace	Jan 27, 1936
16.	George Wagner	Jun 12, 1936
17.	Willie Buffkins	Mar 2, 1936
18.	Ada Robinson	Jan 27, 1937

Former Saints of the Mother Church at Omaha, NE, 1940's & 50's

19.	Irving Green	Mar 1, 1937
20.	Edward Robinson	Mar 2, 1937
21.	Mary Wright	Jun 1, 1937
22.	Josephee Robinson	May 1938
23.	Charles Arnold	Sept 1938
24.	Sic Williams	Nov 2, 1938
25.	Lean McClarity	May 9, 1939
26.	Mattie Bell	Nov 15, 1940
27.	Leroy Wright	Oct 26, 1942
28.	Samuel Charles	Nov 29, 1943
29.	Louis Johnson	May 19, 1943
30.	Jennie Hayden	May 17, 1945
31.	Joseph Chaney	Aug 28, 1944
32.	Walter Pierce	Sept 29, 1945
33.	Lizzie Robinson	Dec 19, 1945
34.	Bessie Buffkins	Sept 13, 1948
35.	Willie McClarity	
36.	Alvin McClarity	Mar 1949[16]

In 1920, the national church created the National Benevolent Burial Association that provided burial insurance specifically for the members of the Church of God in Christ.

Further Expansion in Omaha

The National president of this association was assistant overseer of Texas, Elder. J. Houston Gallaway. He worked to legislate this insurance for several states in the brotherhood, developing this insurance for Church of God in Christ members only. Dad and Mother Robinson purchased this burial plot, and the mother church purchased this burial insurance in its formative years.[11]

The National Benevolent Burial Association

of The Church of God in Christ

CERTIFICATE

1922 Official Certificate COGIC Burial Association

As the congregation grew some of the new converts went to South Omaha, and a new meeting started that meet with great success. The South Omaha meetings witnessed remarkable growth, as people were hungry for the Pentecostal experience. The one meeting turned into two meetings that, in a couple of years, developed into two of the earlier churches in the South Omaha area. Both of the great early South Omaha evangelistic campaigns started similarly as the mother church, on vacant lots with people passing by hearing the gospel of the New Testament experience of speaking in tongues, and the result that many new converts came to Christ.

A church site was started at 30th N.E. corner of V Street, and the other church was located at the corner of 25th S.E. corner of Q Street. Omaha had a lot of industrial packing plants, and many people came from work along these streets and stopped off to hear about the New Testament experience of speaking in other tongues. Many converts came to Christ in the South Omaha area; five churches developed over a period of five years. By 1935, it was documented in the Omaha cross-city directory that:

- In 1928, 2712 R Street became the present day Mt. Zion Church of God in Christ.
- The Rev. W.D. Smith located at 5212 R.

(Center) Bishop Bradford, Elder Holcomb, Elder Alexander

Saints of NE in 1950's & 60's

In 1931 the Rev. Harold P. Fisher located at 3006 V Street.

- In 1932 the Rev. Jessie N. Allen, parents of the late State Mother Lois Price located 1016 S. 13th.
- In 1934, 1208 S. 13th, lived D.M. Watson, Grandparents of State Mother Louise Secret
- In 1926 the Rev. George Hayden located at 5623 S 30th.
- In 1935 the Rev. Gilbert D. Benson, 1710 N. 25th in North Omaha became the present day New Bethel Church of God in Christ. [12]

These are some of the beginning churches, pastors and locations before the mid-forties. Pastor and Mother Robinson lived with Deacon Archie Baker and their daughter Ida Baker who rented the address 2864 Corby. They later, in 1924, purchased this property from Mr. Hansen, which was recorded from Omaha's deed of records. They called this home the big house. This was where Bishop Mason and most national officials stayed when they traveled through Omaha to visit Lizzie. As Mother Robinson continued to travel, some of the spiritual daughters she trained and appointed as state mothers, and her daughter Ida Baker, became her traveling companions. Ida became known as, and was the first person to be called "Big Sister". Ida had a gifted singing ability that cheered the crowds as her mother taught the unadulterated word of God. Lizzie kept a very rigorous traveling schedule, stopping off at every church in the brotherhood to encourage the Prayer and Bible Bands or to establish Sewing Circles in the local churches. [17]

Pastor & Mother Robinson followed in the footsteps of the organizational strategies of Bishop Mason, who was known for legally incorporating his national work. They

L-R Elder Alexander, Bishop B.T. McDaniel and wife, 1940's

Bishop Monty J. Bradford and Elder Robert Alexander

decided early on to organize the mother church of Omaha, Nebraska. Dad Robinson let Mother Robinson know while she was touring the United States that he was ready to hold the first business meeting to incorporate the mother church on July 3, 1925. Lizzie was in St. Paul, Minnesota in July, and she came back to Omaha to attend the business meeting with the members of their five-year-old growing congregation. On July 3, 1925 they set up legal articles of incorporation that, later on, August 3, 1925, at 1:30 p.m. were filed with Frank Dewey, Douglas County Clerk of Nebraska.

Below are the articles of incorporation listing the main members of the mother church of Omaha.

ARTICLES OF INCORPORATION
OF CHURCH OF GOD IN CHRIST OF OMAHA NEBRASKA

Be it remembered that on the 3rd day of July 1925, the majority of the following named persons assembled at the Church building at 2318 North 26th Street Omaha, Nebraska. To-wit, Rev. E. D. Robinson, Lizzie Robinson, Martha Roberson, Ida Baker, E. Chambers, Erma B. Chambers, Douglas Chambers, Malcomb Chambers (Married Lillian Swift; there children were Bobbie, Nettie, Eddie, Gilbert, and Alice, all Chambers), E. Benson, G.D. Benson, A. Cheney, Alice Cheney, Daisey Lane, Sis. Burnell, Lillie Swift (Erie Chamber Mother), Benjamin Stewart, Anna Copeland, Carrie Frontroy, M. Ford (Mother Ford was a recorder or record keeper of the business of the church, her and her husband were prosperous), Jim Ford, Fannie Roberts, Irene Brooks, Ellen Turner, Flora Lewis, Helen Brown, Lillian Williams, Magnulia Nunn, J. L. Nunn, Carrie Ruffin, Walter Ruffin,

Omaha Saints in 1960's

Mother Church Omaha, Nebraska 1947

Pastor England Holcomb of the Mother Church

majority of whom being then and there present, the following proceeding were had with reference to organization and incorporation of said church. Rev. E. D. Robinson was elected Chairman of said meeting and Magnolia Nunn was elected secretary of said meeting. [18]

The congregation that night made the following resolutions:

1. Pastor E. D. Robinson was elected chairman of Corporation.
2. Sis. Magnolia Nunn was elected as church secretary.
3. Name of the church was to be CHURCH OF GOD IN CHRIST
4. There shall be elected from members of the church three not more than five to a Trustee Board.
5. There shall be elected from members of the church four not more than six to a Deacon Board.
6. The board of trustees will manage the church property.
7. There shall be a Treasurer selected of the membership of the church.
8. The first to be elected as Trustees were Douglas Chamber, Archie Baker, and Benjamin Stewart.
9. The first elected Deacons were J.L. Nunn, W.N. Ruffin, Montgomery, and J.D. Benson.
10. Mrs. Magnolia Nunn was elected as Clerk
11. Mrs. C. B. Cheney was elected as treasurer.[18]

Mother's Travel Schedule

Lizzie realized that the national church needed her support. In the early years the women's ministry of the organization, she raised nearly 1/3 of the funds that advanced Bishop Mason's national vision. As the amount of attendees

1939 Convocation, Memphis, TN

for the national meeting always exceeded the space capacity in Memphis, TN, Mason was already making plans to construct a national temple ten times the size of the initial Wellington Street address. The prophecy God gave him was coming true, that there would not be room enough to hold the people attending each year at Holy Convocation. In 1921, he purchased a large plot of land at 958 S. 5th Street for $40,000. His attorney and his founding elders negotiated a land contract deal where the payments for the land would be $10,000 per year until paid. In the mean time, the new national temple was being constructed and the first service at this site was at the 18th Annual Holy Convocation in 1924.

Mother Robinson's women's department established precedence for the future that may not have been available otherwise. She is the one individual that through skillful national appeals to her female constituency brought all of Mason's financial goals over the top. Whatever the men did to support their founding father's vision, her spiritual Deborah's were on the frontlines making sure the need was met. Mother Robinson, with God's divine hand at the helm, manifested through her fund-raising ability and organizational skills, solidified and carved into history in Twentieth-century Pentecostalism, the importance of the role of women in working along side great men of God in ministry.

Mason made a God-given decision, in 1911, to allow a woman to be a national representative of women's ministry with one of the fastest growing Protestant denominations in the history of America in the early part of the twentieth-century. Mason's decision enjoyed results that produced the fastest growing denomination in America's

1932 Saints arriving at Convocation in Memphis, TN

history. What most traditional denominations accomplished in 200 years; his had accomplished in half the time. All of this phenomenal growth was done under an experience of critical scrutiny by the more established Christian denominations. They viewed the phenomena of women on the frontlines as heralding this new Pentecostal experience. Mason was ridiculed and insulted as the man who only had a church full of women. But he held fast to God's revelation to the blood of Christ that he witnessed in 1906 at Azusa Street; that the blood washed away the sexist line that American religious society had formed.

In order to understand the intense travel schedule maintained by Lizzie, year after year, for fourteen years, we can view her intense travel schedule of 1925, and her personal testimony given in a report to the national church:

1. She left Memphis, TN December 16, 1925 from the 18th Holy Convocation to Brinkley, Arkansas.
2. Conducted a winter prayer meeting for Elder Bowe at Geridge, Arkansas the week before Christmas.
3. In January 25, 1925 returned home to Omaha, NE to be with her family.
4. In April 5, 1925 was teaching for Elder O.T. Jones in Ft. Smith, Arkansas. Elder Jones and his wife give Mother Robinson a surprise sixty-fifth birthday party with gifts of a $25.00 toilet set and a cake with sixty-five pink candles.
5. In mid-April she returned to Memphis, TN after hearing about Elder Fredrick's death.
6. On April 29th she attended Elder McEwen's Convocation in Union City, TN.
7. In July 1925 she left St. Paul, Minnesota to return back to Omaha, NE to attend and participate in the incorporation of the mother Church of Nebraska.

8. She was called back to Little Rock, Arkansas to attend her older, ninety-two years old, brother's funeral.[11]

Mother Robinson's Report--1925

I beg leave to make my annual report for the year 1925. Leaving the meeting, my first stop Brinkley, Ark. Elder Hal Mitchell in charge. Found them going on nicely with the work, on to Stuttgart. Elder Welch was in charge at that time. They were busy rallying to get means together to build a new temple. On to Geridge School. Held the mid-winter prayer meetings for one week. Geridge is a fine school, in a beautiful place, away from all evil environments of the city. We found Elder Justus Bowe doing his best to establish a great Holiness School that will be a credit to the Church of God in Christ. Let us send our children to the Holiness School. Try Geridge. Go on Elder Bowe, Arkansas will cause the other states that have no school to wake up when they see what Geridgee is doing.

From there to Little Rock, Arkansas. Elder Welch in charge and that shouting church was praising God as they always do.

1940, 958 5th St, National Temple, Memphis TN

To North Little Rock. Elder J. Bowe in charge. The saints were striving to recover themselves after the storm of the false prophet had blown over.

Visited the East End Mission. Elder Allen was pastor at the time. Also South Temple in Little Rock. They were going on as best they could, not having a pastor at that time. Left for home January 26. Found Elder Robinson and little flock marching on to victory. Brother Crawford and Brother Smith of the south Side on the firing line for the King.

Left home March 23. Kansas City two nights at First Temple. Elder V.M. Barker pastor and overseer. Always seems like a little state convocation here. Visited Brother Brown and Brother Smith. Of course, they are coming right along in the steps of the Mother church. They are wide-awake ministers. Over to Kansas City, Kansas. Brother Young, pastor. Found the children with victory in their souls. From there to Coffeyville, Kansas. The saints there were shouting victory in the new basement of their church. Elder O. T. Jones in charge. Wherever he is head of anything he will surely make it go. Stopped at Nowata, Oklahoma. Some more of Brother Jones' children going on in the strength of the Lord, but with sorrow in their hearts because they did not want to give up their beloved pastor. On to Tulsa. Now you all know who is at Tulsa--Elder J.W. Strasner. He is alive and his children are the same.

To Ft. Smith again. We find Elder O.T. Jones in charge and at home as he was living there at that time. Stayed there five *days. On the fifth of April, in teaching a lesson, I said this is my birthday, I am sixty-five years old today, and to my surprise Elder and Sister Jones asked me my whole name and when I was born, and on Tuesday after I taught the lesson the saints rendered one of the most beautiful programs about Mother I ever witnessed and gave me a $25 toilet set, a cake with sixty-five pink candles on it. How I thanked the Lord for these sweet children who remembered me on my birthday. Just like O.T. and wife. Went from Ft. Smith to Hot Springs. There twelve days. Elder J. Bowe in charge, with Elder Owens assistant. Hot Springs is alive and the saints are on the firing line.*

Stopped a few days in Brinkley with my sister. As we were going to the station on our way to Memphis, TN, the sad news of Elder C.C. Frederick's death came to me. Elder Frederick was one among the greatest in the Church of God in Christ, a man who made friends with every one, who never failed to tell the sinner of his sins, be he black or white, rich or poor, he never at any time gave Elder Mason one minute's trouble or failed to answer to every call of the church. He had one of the best charges in the united work, was liked in Pittsburgh, his home, by all who knew him. "Oh, God, give us more pastors like him." Sleep on, Elder Frederick, we will meet you in the city of the "New Jerusalem.

We were so very sad on our trip to Memphis. There we found Elder S.T. Samuel in a great revival. We were distressed and grieved when we found that we could not get a train in time to be in Pittsburgh to the funeral. Just at this time Elder Samuel came in the room, went down on his knees asking God to comfort, lifts the burden off our hearts, and eases our troubled minds. The Lord came in power and in shadow of death the sunlight of God' s countenance shone upon us. Amen.

From Memphis to Union City, TN., April 29. State Convocation, the best one I ever met in the state of Tennessee. Elder McEwen, overseer, Elder G.A. Sparks, assistant, Mother Alice Clay and her co-workers as helpmeets, carried the work over the top. Elders McEwen and Sparks cut off all the dead limb preachers who keep their names on the list and sit at home doing nothing for the cause of Christ. The meeting was beautiful in spirit and in truth the business was transacted business way any the money above the expenses was put in the bank, not slothful in business, fervent in spirit serving the Lord. Space will not permit me to give an itemized account of all the happenings of the meetings visited.

From St. Louis, MO., to Lexington. On to Kansas City, MO. Out to Denver, Colorado., Oakland, San Francisco, Fresno, and Los Angeles. Down to Phoenix, Arizona.

Up to St. Paul and Minneapolis, MN. Back to Omaha for five days. Down to Dallas, Texas., Oklahoma City, Oklahoma. Topeka, Wichita, Kansas. Kansas City, St. Louis, MO., to Mound City, Ill. Henderson, Ky., up to Milwaukee, Wisconsin. Chicago, Ill., Detroit, Michigan., Buffalo, NY. One night in Philadelphia, PA. On to Norfolk, VA. Back up to Washington, DC To Trenton, N.J. Stopped one night in Harrisburg to see sweet little Jessie Simon. On to Pittsburgh, PA. To Cleveland, Ohio, Toledo. Back to Detroit, Ypsilanti, Michigan., Gary, Indiana., Chicago, Decatur, Ill., St. Louis, and MO. Home again for eleven days. Was called to Little Rock for the death of my brother, who was ninety-two years old. Stopped at Brinkley, Arkansas. Rested here until the meeting of the most wonderful convocation that we have ever had in the history of the Church of God in Christ. Pray on and move on, and the time won't be long. Pray for me that I fight the fight of faith. [11]

Yours truly,
11/25/1925
Mother Lizzie Robinson

SISTER ANNA SMITH
General Recording Secretary

Mrs. Anna Smith

Bishop Mason appointed, in 1922, Mrs. Anna Smith, a member of Elder V.M. Barker's church of Kansas City, Missouri, to be his National Recording Secretary. Mother Robinson was very familiar with Anna's ability, since she often traveled through Missouri to visit the mother church of Missouri. She saw Sister Anna Smith's writing ability and faithfulness to Elder V.M. Barker, Overseer of Western Missouri, Iowa, and Nebraska, and recommended her. Anna Smith later became the National General Recording Secretary of the Church of God in Christ in the early 1920's. One of the important contributions of her life was that she was a female spiritual scribe, because she personally dictated by hand word-for-word the earlier sermons of Bishop C.H. Mason at the National Holy Convocation from 1920-1945. Even though there was no electronic device to record these earlier messages her dictation remained the most detailed account of his early public presentations. Here is part of one of her dictations on December 1926 in Memphis, TN. The title of the message was called Storms.

Sermon in Part
By Elder C.H. Mason
By Anna Smith, General Recording Secretary
Sermon Title Storms

> *The Lord will have His way in the storms, and the clouds are the dust of His feet. Nahum 1:2-3 talk of His wonders and make known His deeds among the people. Ps. 105:1. Some of the wise of today are saying God has nothing to do with the storm. However, the Bible says: he Lord will have His way in the whirlwinds and in the storms.*

God will rise up as in Mount Perazim and be wroth as in the Valley of Gibeon, that He may do His work, His strange work, and bring to pass His strange acts. Isaiah 28:21. The word says that he proud and the drunkards shall be visited of the Lord of host, with thunder and earthquakes and great noise, with storm and tempest, and the flame of devouring fire. Isaiah 29:86. God with the hand of the storm shall cast down to the earth: proud folks and God shall trample them under His foot in the storm. Nahum 1:2-3, Isaiah 28:1-3.[5]

Below is Anna's overview of the Eighteen Annual Convocation of 1925:

Anna Smith, Recording Secretary, and Residence: 2029 Flora, Kansas City, Missouri.

The saints of God in Christ from all parts of the United States, extending into British West Indies, have again come together and ended one of the greatest Annual Convocations in the history of the Church, both spiritual and financial. The spirit of the Lord drawing us together in a man, in himself could not accomplish. Truly God was in the midst of his people blessing them in purpose and will to stand as never before in the council of God.

The three days consecration was sweet to all who went through, and God was glorified. How the fire did fall. God's healing

> *power was greatly manifested. We welcome Elder S.T. Samuel, of North Carolina, and Elder S.H. Jones, of St. Louis, both of whom God has blessed with faith in healing. They taught faith by the word of God to the sick, prayed and anointed them and they in turn caught more faith and many left their crutches to be hung up as a memorial and went on their way healed, and rejoicing in the God of their salvation. Others healers were present in the person of Elder F.W. McGee, of Iowa, and Elder J.E. Morris, of Colorado, all working in one accord for the healing of bodies. Tumors were dried up, an ulcerated leg healed. One who had been paralyzed for years walked. The blind said: OW I SEE, Saints claimed the victory over many diseases of years standing, the blood covering all who believed.* [11]

Anna's writings stand as an important record of the early events of messages that took place during the national holy convocation. Many of her dictations were lost, but ten to fifteen are recorded in the 1926 yearbook for the 15th Holy Convocation.

Anna also documented the order of services for the National convocation; here is her listing of sermons, songs, and conductors of divine healing service in 1925, November 25-December 15, during the 18th Holy Convocation held in Memphis, TN.

Order of Services

Conducted 3 day fast prior to Convocation: Elder C.H. Mason

Conducted Daily 9:00am Pray: Elder S.T. Samuel

Sermons

1. Elder S. Rice, Overseer, Mississippi; Title: "*If He Delights in us, then He Will Bring us into His Land, so Fear Them Not*"; Text: Numbers 14:8-9.
2. E. M. Wilson, Overseer of California; Title: *Who Must Be Born Again?*" Text: John 3:5.
3. Chief Apostle C.H. Mason; Title: "*Take Heed to Yourselves and to the Flock of God over Which the Holy Ghost has Made You Overseer to Feed the Church of God, Which He has Purchased With His Own Blood*"; Text: Acts 20:28.
4. Elder R. Williams, Overseer of Alabama; Title: *The Power and Endurance of Love* Text: I John 3:1.
5. Elder R.W. Weiner, Michigan; Title: "*The Immutability of God*"; Text: Hebrews 6:17, Psalms 50:2.
6. Chief Apostle C.H. Mason; Title: *Beware of Dogs*"; Text: Philippians 3:2.
7. Elder R. Williams, Overseer of Alabama; Title: *Well of Water Spring up into Everlasting Life*"; Text: Isaiah 35: 1-8.
8. Elder H. Gallaway, Texas; Title: *The Ministry of Reconciliation* Text: 2 Corinthians 5:14.
9. Elder Chief Apostle C.H. Mason; Title: "*Only a Kept Vessel is fit for leadership.*"
10. Elder Chief Apostle C.H. Mason; Title: "*We Are Examples of the Compassion of Christ in the Flesh*"; Text: 2 Tim 4:1-2, John 20:23.
11. Elder Austin Love, Texas; Title: "*Shall We Continue In Sin That Grace May Abound? God Forbid.*"
12. Chief Apostle C.H. Mason; Title: "*O Ye Dry Bones Hear the Word of the Lord*";
Text: Ezekiel 37:4:5.

13. Elder Nesbit, Cocoa, Florida; Title: "*Catch The Fox*"; Text: Song of Solomon 2:15.
14. Elder A.L. Gilliam, Kansas; Title: "*This Thing*"; Text: Deut. 4:32, Luke 1:35.

Lessons Taught

1. General Mother Lizzie Robinson; Topic: *Personal Work* Scriptures: John 4:1.
2. General Mother Lizzie Robinson; Topic: *Evolution* Text: Gen. 1:21, Rom. 1:20.
3. Elder J.E. Hightower, Mariana & Elder Charles Pleas, Parsans, Kansas- Describes the life and work of Apostle C.H. Mason's Life.
4. Elder S.H. Jones, of St. Louis, MO; Topic: D*ivine Healing* Text: Mark 9:23.
5. Elder F.C. Christmas, National Superintendent Sunday School; Topic: "*Paul Before Agrippa*"; Golden Text: "*I Was Not Disobedient to the Heavenly Vision*"; Acts 26:19; Practical Truth: *Great Vision Calls for a Great Work.*"
6. General Mother Lizzie Robinson; Topic: Soldier's *Armor* Text: Ephesians 6:11-18.
7. General Mother Lizzie Robinson; Topic: "*Women's Place in the Church*"; Text: Joel 2:28-29, Mica 6:4, Exodus 15:20, 2 Kings 22:14-20, Luke 8:1-3, Acts 9:36, Acts 18:1-4, 2 Samuel 16-20.
8. Elder F.C. Christmas, National Superintendent Sunday School; Topic:" *The Christian Overcoming Adverse Criticism*"; Golden Text: Matt. 14:27.

Songs Sung

1. Twin Sister Rhetha and Letha Morris they sang, "*Who is That Writing John, the Revelator*?"
2. Elder S. Rice, Overseer, Mississippi, "*Thou Cares Lord.*"

3. General Mother Lizzie Robinson, "*No Man Can Do Me Like Jesus.*"
4. General Mother Lizzie Robinson, "*Happy Day, When Jesus Washed My Sins Away.*"
5. Elder E.M. Page, Overseer of California, "*I Want to be Like Jesus in my Heart.*"
6. Elder F.C. Christmas, National Superintendent Sunday School, "*No, Not One.*"
7. Elder R. Williams, Overseer of Alabama, "*There will be no night there.*"
8. Elder Chief Apostle C.H. Mason, "*God's Will. be Done.*"
9. Elder F.C. Christmas, National Superintendent Sunday School, "*Leaning on The Everlasting Arms.*"

Divine Healers and miracles during Alter Services Salvation & Baptism in Holy Ghost

1. Elder Chief Apostle C.H. Mason
2. Elder S.T. Samuels, of North Carolina
3. Elder S.H. Jones, of St. Louis, MO
4. Elder F.W. McGee, of Iowa
5. Elder J.E. Morris, of Colorado
6. W.G. Shipman, Detroit, Michigan
7. Elder J. Felters, Louisiana[11]

1946 Memphis Convocation, Elder C. G. Brown (Center of Picture)

Sis. Green (she was Indian) Hens Bates, Zelee Williams, Bettie Williams, A. McGill (they only had girls, a lot of girls, 5 or 6 girls, we used to play with her baby daughter - she was spoiled. She had a doll that walked. We used to like to go to her house cause we liked to play with her toys), Fannie Williams, Mary Mitchell, Anna Turner, Susie Archie, Mattie Cooper (They later left the mother church to start another church, they had allot of children, New Bethel, the Cooper's took elder Allen's church), Hattie Bell (she was related to elder Halcomb, when they had a barn across the street where they cooked food she was in charge of the selling of food during the convocation. (the place where she took charge of the cooking looked like a garage), Glutethia Taylor (later married Elder Holcomb, Gulethia Taylor, Elder Holcomb gave his testimony that who he had was not his wife, he married Gulethia, mother Guletha died in the church. She picked out his wife. Mother Guletha picked out his wife before she died. She went to Bishop Bradford, said she knew that God was going to take her, she did not know what to do about England Holcomb, so she picked out his wife. The church, allot of times in those days, arranged the marriages. Elder Holcomb said he was glad he did not marry this other woman. He worked over to Packing House. He worked at Armors Packing houses off of Q. St.-Amours, Cudahy, and Swift Packing House), Ernest Swift, Alice Swift (The uncle and aunt of Lillian Swift, Became Lillian Chambers), Dorene Marshall, Georgia Scaggs, Elizabeth Martin, E. D. Willis, Mary Martin, Lula Burrell, Sis. Ellison, Artie Hughes, A. Baxter, John Whitby, Dane Byas, Martha Yancy, Jennie Hill, Lillian Roberson, John Montgomery, Jessie Montgomery, Julia Washington, Leslie Stewart, Sis Burt, Jack Hicks, Lillian Swift, forty four (44) of the above named members being present. Who constitute the members and incorporators of CHURCH OF GOD IN CHRIST of Omaha, Nebraska, the

Testimony of Bishop Mason

Another significant individual that was saved and received the baptism of the Holy Ghost at the first revival on 21st and Flora was Elder C.G. Brown. He was one of the founding members of Elder Barker's revival in 1917. Elder C.G. Brown was also a noted writer surrounding the early life and observations of Bishop C.H. Mason. The Midwestern states held true to the church as the place where very significant individuals resided, among who were writers and authors that observed and documented early history. Sister Anna Smith and C.G. Brown of Kansas City, Missouri, who were saved under the ministry of young Elder V. M. Barker, were gifted to write and document Mason's ministry. Many people in the Mason movement were so amazed at his works that they did not think about recording things for future generations to be reminded of his great works.

Below is her personal testimony concerning Mason's significance, the unity of the church, his revelations, his prayer life, and his extraordinary Psalmist and worship ministry. She specifically left on record his allowing the women to work within his Church, allowing them to travel with him, and read the scriptures and sing before he taught the word. Here is her statement, that of record written around the time she was soon to be promoted from her labor to reward.

> *I traveled on the road with Brother Mason and older Sisters. I sang and read the Bible as he preached, as we always did in those days. He influenced me and saw to it that I read the Bible once a year. I was blessed to sit for hours under his tutorship. I worked as a secretary in his office for*

twenty-one years. Part of the time I assisted Sister Jesse Strickland who was then Financial Secretary. I held that office until I was made National Mother.

I stood by in those hours when he was slowly leaving us and prayed out of my broken heart for God to leave this Great Man with us. One whom I had seen prophecy and his prophesies came to pass. Long before radio and television was known of, he told us that we would stand here and be heard and seen to the ends of the world. Yes and in addition to all this, he sang thousands of songs. Oh, if we had only had ears to hear and have written his songs. It seemed that we did not realize that he would leave us some day. He counseled as no other man I have ever heard. Few of his sons have left the church under his administration. I have seen him go in where there was great confusion, and pray for hours and hours. When he got up, the trouble was all over. He loved his sons and his daughters. He always kept some of his daughters near him and would let the women of God work in the church and make use of our God given talents. [19]

Below are some of C.G. Brown's observation of Mason's spiritual vibrancy that caused people to wonder after his ministry in those earlier days:

Observations of Elder C.H. Mason, Chief Apostle, 1918.
By Elder C.G. Brown 2029 Flora Ave., Kansas City, Missouri.

Oh to hear him pray is to be elevated with the confidence that he is always in communion with the Father and that he is under the influence of the Holy Ghost who knows how to pray for himself (Elder Mason), for others and for that (The Church of God) which has been committed to his leadership. His request are made in such a manner as to be awe-inspiring and to make one fed that to have such a character pray for him is to know that he will receive an answer to his petition weather it is encouraging or discouraging, whether it is for life more abundantly a promotion in God or a "taking away from the earth."

The following are some of priceless treasures of the Spirit's praying through him. "Father I am thankful to Thee because Thou makest me love Thee. In thy wonder fulfilling I am with thee. Lets all live in the fear of God and let the water of thy word quicken all, for we are no more aliens but the sons of God, "born of his wonder." Move distress from the hearts of thy servants. Let the signs be wrought in the land and the gospel of Jesus Christ is confirmed in souls everywhere, for thou art worthy of all. Father these are thine, when we come for help we are thine. Hear the groans and let them say, I will. We thank God for His way in the temple and pray God rebuke the wicked. Favor thy children with thyself and let thy name be mighty. Heal children bodies and let them know they must be healed. Great is God. Give these the strength of the word. Forgive and let these be forgiven. Let the wonder of thy way heal all and the wicked shall be subject to your will. Help, Jesus with thy word, with Christ the Conqueror. Comfort these that mourn and bind the evil spirit in Jesus name. Give me speak in the Holy Ghost. Amen. Let these who draw nigh to God keep the mind of His greatness. Lord Christ anoints these and delivers them from what is evil. Comfort the feeble and let the kingdom come in their minds. "Bless us with thy loving tenderness, the beauty of Christ be upon these, comforting them with thyself. Come into these in the Holy Ghost. Break forth in their souls and govern in the earth.

Spiritual singing is another manner in which God expresses Himself through him. By it evil spirits are driven away and souls are called to repentance. When he arises to sing under the influence of the Spirit, the glory of God envelops him and his soul is consumed in the sweetness of God's love. The music is so melodious and full of harmony, the thought is so blessed and full of inspiration and with such heavenly comfort, the words are so selected and well phased that those who know Christ and have been baptized into His body, realized that God has furnished His servant with an invisible song book upon whose pages are written songs to subdue every human passion, to extol the name of Jesus, to exalt the way of God, and supply a balm for every wound and a cordial for every fear. Very often the power of God is glorious manifested through the singing that the assemblies of the saints are aroused with the same fire of enthusiasm and take up the theme and sing together with him till they are carried to heights unknown to the natural mind. Having come before God's presence with singing, the soul cries after more knowledge and lifts up its voice for understanding, it seeks for it as silver and searches for it as for hidden treasury. It shall then understand the fear of the Lord, wisdom then enters the heart and know is pleasant to the soul. As the Holy Ghost increases the spirit of the Psalmist in him, he soars higher and higher in God's delight and takes God's children with him. If the billows and storms of life have assailed them, if varied afflictions have burdened their souls, there is always a peaceful calm and a sweet relief, when the Spirit has finished its singing through him.

Order and Governance for the Women's Work

Mother Robinson traveled, continuously mothering the small churches within Mason's organization. She was the most visible national official working in the trenches to make sure each Pastor and State Supervisor in the brotherhood had her on-hand support. Her national concern for the growth of the local church went beyond each state women's ministry, for instance, as stated, she held prayer meetings, taught Bible lessons, ran revivals and raised funds. Lizzie, through the virtues of itinerate travel, kept her ear to the ground, so that she knew the issues of the local pastors and state mothers surrounding women in ministry.

This established protocol later became a part of the corporate culture of the Church of God in Christ, The fourth National Mother stated these words at her National Women's Meeting, "*Some women want to come to the national church to work without doing their homework.*" She meant, that like school, you would not have success later without doing your studying at home. It is the same principle involved in the church. If you have not been faithful getting any of your work done in your local state organization, how can you be successful on the national level? You cannot jump from the local level, not respecting your local governing body, to be effective nationally. What you do locally will reflect nationally; so she felt you should work it out at the lower level first, then you do not have to have the same problems by the time God brings you to serve nationally.

Mother Robinson realized that the department of women had taken on a very prominent role from the time she started it fifteen years prior to 1911. The Bible Bands, Home and Foreign Mission Bands, and the local women's departments she developed in the formative years began to become a platform to uplift women's spiritual leadership development and their sociological growth in Bishop Mason's organization. As more women accepted their calling to rise up and go to the frontlines of ministry by fasting and prayer meetings, and becoming a witness for Christ, they became the nets prepared to draw in the great harvest of souls witnessed in the organization's formative years.

Reflected over the fruitful fifteen years of her work within the organization, Mother Robinson wanted to establish protocol and governance for the many females that had come out of the shadows of obscurity to impact their local communities with the gospel of Jesus Christ. Along with much growth came problems, when individuals become overzealous to the point of not wanting to be governed, which was an insult to Mother Robinson's first vision of the women's work? She did not want Satan to take occasion to be able to falsely accuse this new army of dry bones rising in service to God's Kingdom. Therefore, in 1926, she adopted rules for the women's work to give direction and guidance to her spiritual daughters to be governed by. These rules were also established for those who said they were sent but actually went on their own without the support and recommendation of their current leadership. Mother Robinson developed these rules out of her experience of hearing the positive and negative responses of the men and women within Mason's organization.

pastor and they will not be permitted to teach if it is found out that she talks with the weaker ones of the church who fight the pastorship.

9 No sister who has two or three husbands unlawfully according to the doctrines of the church of God in Christ can be a Missionary.

10 Workers requesting some sister to work, send your request to your pastor or State Mother.

11 All sisters applying for License to do Missionary Work must come before the State Mother's Board with recommendations from their pastor.

12 These rules are to be read in Bible Board Meetings.

All members and all Missionaries in good and regular standing with the Church of God in Christ must work in unity with the State Overseer, State Mother and Pastor.

ELDER C. H. MASON, Senior Bishop
MOTHER LIZZIE ROBINSON
General Supervisor of Women's Work

RULES
of the
WOMEN'S WORK
†
of the
Church of God in Christ

1926, National Rules for Women's Work, Memphis. TN

Mother Robinson foresaw the importance of having order and governance. With the spiritual gifts of women developing at an extraordinary pace she needed to establish rules for the women's work. She realized that by doing this she would be setting a strong foundation for the future of women's ministry, and separate the wise virgins from the foolish. This would also help new converts not to follow behind those that would led them astray under the pretense that they were doing a work for God, but could not prove their ministry by being subject to their local leaders. Mother Robinson understood that the phenomenal growth of her "Spiritual Deborah's" would become an object of critical scrutiny within and beyond her organization. Therefore, she carved out protocol for this new army so they would know how to relate amongst leadership at the local level. Mother Lizzie Robinson wrote the first set of official rules for the women's ministry in 1925, which was adopted December 15, 1926 at the fifteenth annual sitting of the women's work in Memphis, Tennessee. Here is what Lizzie wrote in her own hand.

RULES FOR THE WOMEN'S WORK

Adopted December 15, 1926 in the 15th Annual sitting of the Women's Work, Memphis, TN.

The following rules for the help of Women's Work in General in the Church of God in Christ under the leadership of the general Mother, Lizzie Robinson, were adopted the 15th day of December, 1926 in the 15th Annual setting of the women's work, Memphis, Tennessee.

1. Members and Missionaries must attend Prayer and Bible Band, Home and Foreign Mission Band and be active in all Women's Auxiliaries in Church and governed by the

(L-R, Front row) Bishop C. H. Mason, Evangelist Reatha Herdon (National Evangelist)

Bishop Mason Validating the Women's Convention 1955

word and obey them that have the rule over them Hebrews 13:17, Luke 6:46.

2. They must themselves be commendable and be recommended by their Prayer and Bible Band leader, Home and Foreign Mission Leaders and Pastors, as faithful workers as Phoebe, Romans 16:1-2.
3. All members and Missionaries are requested to pay Tithes and Offerings, according to scriptures, Mal. 3:8-10, Nehemiah 13:12, Matt 23:23, Luke 11:42. They must be faithful in paying each assessment, and attending service in their own church.
4. All members and Missionaries must dress in modest apparel and becometh holiness, professing Godliness with good work.
5. All members and Missionaries must not wear hats with flowers or feathers, nor short sleeves. Young Missionaries, who have a desire or gift to do Missionary Work, should go to the aged or more experienced women.
6. That no young Missionary go here and there with any Elder or Brother to do Missionary Work without consulting their State Mother and Pastor.
7. Any sister applying for License to do Missionary Work having left her home church and is worshipping in another, should get a letter of recommendation from her Pastor at home to the church in which she worships.
8. All Missionaries holding meetings must first consult the pastor and they will not be permitted to teach if it is found out that she talks with the weaker ones of the church who fight the pastorship.
9. No sister who has two or three husbands unlawfully according to the doctrines of the church of God in Christ can be a Missionary.

10. Workers requesting some sister to work, send your request to your pastor or State Mother.
11. All sisters applying for License to do Missionary Work must come before the State Mother's Board with recommendations from their pastor.
12. These rules are to be read in Bible Board Meetings. All members and all Missionaries in good and regular standing with the Church of God in Christ must work in unity with the State Overseer, State Mother and Pastor.[19]

Elder Searcy and the Seeds of International Mission

In Lizzie's overall national work she had institutionalized several programs from the time of her appointment in 1911. She started out first with the prayer and Bible Band organizing it in every local church in the United States within Bishop Mason's organization. The next phase was the sewing circle, encouraging women to become involved with uplifting the economic environment within their households. The establishment of a national network of women leaders, known as state supervisors, assisted the bishop in every state within Mason's organization. The autonomy that was given to her ministry placed the women in a pivotal position to also develop the global vision of Mason's organization. For example, while Mother Robinson was touring the United States she met an Elder Searcy in Portland, Oregon, who had an organization with a vision to implement a Home and Foreign Mission organization. Lizzie saw the need to bring this global vision of ministry into the fold of the Church of God in Christ. She was instrumental in organizing the meeting with Mason and Elder Searcy in Memphis, TN in 1925.[9]

1955, Tubake, Africa, first girls dormitory built by Missionary Beatrice Lott of Dallas, Texas

Chapter 6

Mother & Her Missionaries Influence the COGIC Global Vision

Lizzie saw the need for Mason to begin to extend his reach beyond the United States to include an organized Home and Foreign Mission component to his church work. As a result of Mother Robinson's recommendation a relationship developed between Mason's organization and Elder Searcy's to implement a Home and Foreign Mission part to his organization. Elder Searcy was made the president of this component while Mother Robinson's sole responsibility was to assist him in implementing and integrating it into Mason's denominational structure. Mason knew that Lizzie was the person to orchestrate this since she had developed three of the major components of his women's ministry. He had great faith in her organizational skills, which had been demonstrated effectively over fifteen years. Everything she touched seemed to prosper in her hands.

In June of 1926, before the vision could unfold, Elder Searcy decided to withdraw his organization from the Church of God in Christ. This separation delayed the global vision that Lizzie desired for Mason's organization. Mother Robinson, with her passion, would not allow this situation to let the vision that God had given her fall to the ground. She

1953, Mary McLeod Bethune and Dr. Arenia Mallory

realized that God wanted Bishop Mason's ministry to extend beyond its national scope. She envisioned an African-American leader affecting the foreign mission fields. Historically almost all of the organizations were white that had missionaries in the foreign fields. Most black organizations did not extend their vision into the foreign fields until thirty or more years later. Many of the white religious organizations would not allow African-Americans to be missionaries in foreign fields. One of the most notable African-American female figures, Mary McLeod Bethune, attended the Moody Bible Institute in Chicago, IL. Her first desire was to be a foreign missionary to Africa, but because of racial bias they turned down her application. They did not feel an African-American should minister in the foreign fields. At this point she turned to being an educator within the United States and later developed Bethune College in Daytona Beach, FL.

Dr. Arenia Mallory and Mary McLeod Bethune

Another great stride for females within Mason's organization occurred when he placed a female over his school in Lexington, Mississippi. Professor James Courts had started the school as its first principle. After his death, Mason prayerfully selected a young lady he met in 1926. She made him aware of her desire to teach at his school in Lexington. Later she left Missouri for Lexington and began to teach at the school.

After Professor Court's death, Mason appointed the young lady as the president of his school in Mississippi. At this time in history, Mary McLeod Bethune was the only African-American female who was over her own school. Mason allowed another open door for a female educator to

Professor James Courts, First principal of Lexington School

have the opportunity within ministry in his denomination to lead out the vision of his organization's school.

In March or April of 1926, Bishop Mason first met Arenia Mallory at the Missouri & Nebraska Ministers and Workers meeting, which convened in Springfield, Missouri. At the time, she was serving as a young missionary under Bishop V.M. Barker's jurisdiction.[7] Mallory was born and reared in Jacksonville, Illinois. She was the daughter of Mr. Edward and Mrs. Mary Brooks Mallory. She received her high school training in Jacksonville, Illinois. She graduated from Whipple Academy, and later received her BA Degree from Simmons College, Louisville, Kentucky. In 1936 she received her Masters Degree in Education from Jackson College, Jackson, Mississippi. She made it known to Mason that her desire was to teach in Africa. Mason encouraged her to go south to Lexington, Mississippi to a poor area that needed help educating youth in his Christian school. He agreed to give her an open door opportunity to make use of her gift to educate the uneducated in Mississippi. She took the divine advice and encouragement of Mason and moved to Lexington to use her God-given teaching skills.

When Arenia got there she saw the great need and began to work. At this time the school had grades ranging from elementary to eighth. Mason had her appointed to work as the assistant principle to Professor James Courts and Miss Pinky Duncan who started the school. Later Bethune and Mallory, who were contemporaries during this era in history, ended up working together within the women's club movement. Dr. Arenia Mallory and Mary McCloud Bethune both started with a desire to be an educator on the shores of the continent of Africa. They both became a vital part of administrating Colleges in the south. Later, in 1935, both of

1946, Memphis, TN, Mary McLeod Bethune attended Mother Coffey's Installation Service as Second General Mother of COGIC

them helped to charter and found The National Council of Negro Women, which Bethune initiated in New York. Mallory was a charter and life member of the National Council of Negro Women and she took the helm as regional director to assist Bethune's organization's foundational growth. She held this position for eight years, during which time she organized the southern regional meetings for Bethune in the states of Alabama, Arkansas, Florida, Louisiana, Mississippi, Oklahoma, and Texas. Dr. Mallory later became the international spokesperson for Bethune, speaking in her place internationally. She was a delegate representing Mary McLeod Bethune at the Council at the Convention of Women in Helsinki, Finland; and immediately following this occasion, she was guest of the Swedish Council of Women in Europe. Her noted acknowledgments through Bethune and many civic organizations were:[24]

1. National Council of Negro Women in 1940, "Outstanding Women of America."
2. National Council of Negro Women in 1956, "Educator and Leader of Women."
3. Bethune Cookman College of Daytona Beach, Florida 1950, awarded the degree of Doctor of Laws.
4. The Utility Club of New York shared honors with Adam Clayton Powell, Jr. as Utility Club's "Man of the Year Award." Dr. Mallory received "Woman of the Year Award."
5. National Council of Negro Women in 1945, selected as one of the twelve Most Outstanding Women in America."
6. National Council of Negro Women selected as First Vice President 1954 & First Vice President on Educational Commission in 1956.

1946, Memphis, TN, Mary McLeod Bethune, honorary guest sitting in the pulpit at Mason Temple

7. United Nations selected as delegate in 1955 at their tenth celebration.
8. The National Negro Business and Professional Women's Clubs 1963 received Sojourner Truth Award.
9. Appointed by Washington, DC during John F. Kennedy's administration as consultant in 1963 for Labor Department involving problems with minorities in unemployment. [24]

Both women traveled throughout the United States, taking a group of their students to conduct musicals to raise funds to sustain their schools. Mrs. Bethune was impressed with the strides of women within Bishop Mason's organization. Bethune felt that the women of the Church of God in Christ were making important historical achievements for African-American women. Mary Bethune knew too well how organized religious denominations allowed their sexist behavior to hold back the opportunities of females within and under the umbrella of religion. She had to go outside of the church to affect her community. She observed the unusual relationship with Bishop Mason to women as an important phenomenon in American women's history. When she started the National Council of Negro Women, it was no wonder why she selected Dr. Mallory as one of the charter members. She saw the Church of God in Christ women as a ready and available national network, organized in every state, that could support the vision of the National Council of Negro Women. Both of these educators worked untiring together to improve the state of African-Americans in America.

Mother Robinson's position with Mason as a national female leader, not only had a vision for the foreign fields, but became instrumental in laying the organizational

Mother Coffey donating the first jeep to the Missionaries of Africa

and financial groundwork for an international program within Mason's denomination. This took place at a time when most African-American females were denied the opportunity to minister in the foreign fields. Within the Pentecostal Movement, there were more white females serving as missionaries in foreign countries, most of them going back to minister to people of their own culture after receiving the Pentecostal experience of the Azusa Street Revival.

The Home and Foreign Mission Board

On December 2, 1926, at Memphis, Tennessee, Mother Robinson persuaded Bishop Mason to create the Home and Foreign Mission component of the Church of God in Christ organization (Searcy's House of Prayer International was accepted as an affiliate of Mason's denomination). Therefore, The National Elders Council of the Church of God in Christ, during its day session, organized a national missionary board to carry out the functions of a global vision for ministry. Mother Robinson recommended to Bishop Mason, Elder C.G. Brown, of Kansas City, Missouri as a good appointment as Executive Secretary & Treasurer. Bishop Mason accepted her suggestion, knowing she would be the main catalyst behind the auxiliaries' success, and that she had a better feel for who would work by her side to see the vision realized. Elder C.G. Brown was an elder that worked with Lizzie's local Bishop in Nebraska, Bishop Barker. Lizzie knew of his faithful work under Bishop Barker and that he would be an excellent candidate to assist her in handling the administration and finances for this program.

At the meeting in Memphis the Elder's Council carved out the purpose and mission of the new Home and Foreign Mission board. Their directive would be to develop an international plan to engage individuals within the church to encourage an interest in the Foreign Field and to stress that missions was an important issue to the overall mission of the Gospel of Jesus Christ. They stated that day, "*Since the work of the Gospel being published among all nations depends upon individual efforts, we believe by prayer and the guidance of the blessed Holy Spirit by precept and example and personal efforts, we may be partakers of the great Cause, for which the Master died, through the cooperative efforts of individuals and a system of Mission Bands in love and unity.*" They also outlined the purpose of the board was to be for the winning of souls to Christ and to establish the work of grace in the hearts of believers, to encourage a holy life and the Baptism of the Holy Ghost and Fire among all nations of the earth, to make ready a people who are walking in the light, with fellowship of Saints. The board consisted of the following five elected members:

1. Elder J.R. Anderson, Far Rockaway, NY, as President
2. Elder V.M. Barker, Kansas City, Missouri, Vice President
3. Elder Charles Pleas, Recording Secretary
4. Elder F.W. McGee, Chicago, Illinois, Corresponding Secretary
5. Mrs. Lula M. Cox, New Jersey, Supervisor Women's Work

The treasury was supported by a system of Home and Foreign Mission Bands that would be organized by Mother Robinson in every church in the brotherhood. The money would be collected from the local bands. Bishop Mason gave her the consent to organize these bands, so they became a part

1st Church built in Monrovia, Africa, 1953

of the women's work of the organization. Therefore, she proceeded to implement the program as she had done in other auxiliaries.[7]

The first individual to respond to volunteer work in a foreign field was Mrs. Mattie McCaulley, of Tulsa, Oklahoma. Where Mary McLeod Bethune was not allowed to serve in the foreign field, the majority of those that were willing to serve in foreign countries were females. Mother Robinson had opened the door for ministry within the United States through Bishop Mason's movement through the doors of international opportunity when they opened under her administration. Only five short years following American women receiving suffrage rights, Lizzie's female army set foot upon foreign soil for the building of God's Kingdom. The first location selected was Trinidad, West Indies. Mrs. McCaulley stayed there for several years establishing Christ in the hearts of the people of that country. Lizzie created considerable autonomy within the organization to develop the global vision of the Churches of God in Christ. From 1927 to 1940, she untiringly toured, developing the Home and Foreign Mission Bands and raising financial contributions through virtual travel.[7]

Lizzie was able to finance several female and male missionaries to establish the work in the foreign fields. She assumed the leadership of the Home and Foreign Mission of the church, again exercising a level of leadership not given to a female, white or black, under male denominational leadership.

First Orphanage built in Haiti, 1955, on porch (L-R) St. Justus and Missionary Dorothy Exhume

Lizzie again placed her male counterpart on the map globally; she was very adamant about supporting such a man that gave her thc freedom to build within God's Kingdom.

Mrs. Mattie McCaulley and the First Foreign Missionaries

Mrs. Mattie McCaulley was the first female to become a foreign missionary for Lizzie's early foreign mission program. When they called for willing volunteers to dedicate and sacrifice their life amongst unfamiliar people, historically, a woman was the first to make this type of sacrifice for God's Kingdom. No men stood up at the convocation to contend for this humbling position; where one would have to leave the comforts of the United States to live amongst the heathen to preach the unadulterated word of God. This was not an easy task, to be the first to fight on the frontlines, forging out new ground, and going where no African-American man or woman had gone before.

When Mattie got to several foreign countries, there was no one to greet her, but she had to make herself welcome, being a stranger in a foreign land. Mrs. McCaulley learned to eat their unfamiliar food and live where they lived in order to win some to Christ. This event marked another important annul in history; that African-American women also founded and established the beginning roots of the Pentecostal faith within Bishop Mason's denomination on foreign grounds. Mrs. McCaulley, after spending some time in Trinidad, transferred to Cristobal, Canal Zone. She planted the faith there for a short time then went to Costa Rica. The following individuals participated in Mother Robinson's Home and Foreign Mission program in the formative years:

Missionary to Africa, Beatrice Lott, lays foundation for Clinic, 1963

1. Mrs. Mattie McCauley, Tulsa, Oklahoma first volunteer missionary went to Trinidad, West Indies, Cristobal, Canal Zone, and Costa Rica.
2. Elder Cornelius Hall, Los Angeles, California volunteered for British West Indies in 1928.
3. Elder RE Handfield, assisted Elder Hall, served in British West Indies until his death 1949.
4. Miss Elizabeth White, in 1930, who had served in Africa under another Pentecostal group volunteered to go back to Cape Palmas, Africa for the Church of God in Christ.
5. Mrs. Willis C. Ragland, of Columbus, Georgia volunteered for Africa to assist Miss White in 1932.
6. Miss Beatrice Lott, of Dallas, Texas volunteered for Africa in 1937.
7. Miss Dorothy Webster of Cleveland, Ohio volunteered for The Republic of Haiti in 1947.
8. Miss Martha Barber volunteered for Africa in 1947.
9. Mrs. Francina Wiggins sent to Africa in 1949.[7]

Mrs. White was the first woman to make headway in the continent of Africa. Mother Robinson was impressed with her former background as a missionary in Africa. She recruited Mrs. White as a vital piece to see the Churches of God in Christ spread to the mainland of Africa. She saw this woman as one who could establish the faith under Bishop Mason's organization. Mother Robinson invited Mrs. White to the convocation to help her get financial backing from the organization to go to Africa. She went to Africa alone in 1930, worked with the natives, and despite the trickery of witchcraft was able to win souls to the Kingdom of God. Mother Robinson received word of her success, and she raised money to send her an assistant, Mrs. Ragland, to Africa.

1965, Bishop Crouch, over Foreign Missions, with representatives from L-R, Haiti, India

In 1932, Mrs. Ragland boarded a ship to join Mrs. White in Africa. Mrs. White returned to the United States to rest in 1935. She toured the United States speaking about the great progress that was being made on the continent of Africa. In 1937, she met another woman who desired to work with her, Miss Beatrice Lott of Dallas, Texas. Both returned to Africa and started a new station in the Tubake, Africa area. The work had grown so well that Mrs. Ragland continued to work in the Bonika Station because of the amount of souls that came to Christ from their past missionary work. She took Miss Lott to another area to develop out a new mission field. Then, after training and organizing the work with Miss Lott in Tubake Station, she undertook another location at the Wisseka Station. God began to prosper the mission field for Miss White, who had two mentors now to help her establish the work there. Eventually, when World War II came, the forces of combat overtook the continent of Africa; so the missionaries came home until things settled.

Pentecostal Worship and Bishop Barker's Band

One area of significance in the Churches of God in Christ was their manner of worship. In most traditional African-American churches playing musical instruments was considered non-spiritual. The Pentecostal faith used all sorts of instruments within their worship experience, and they seemed to break all the rules of the main line religious faiths. Not only did they attract others from traditional religions to see their speaking in tongues and dancing in the spirit, but they also used all sorts of musical instruments along with the worship experience.

The holiness church, as they were called by traditional religious organizations, would refer to their style

Orchestra in Chicago, IL, 1955, COGIC

of worship if they wanted a traditional congregation to become more expressive in how they worshipped God. One of the famous sayings the Rev. James Cleveland used in the traditional Baptist faith was, I wish I were in a holiness church, to provoke the Baptists to move from slow-paced movement in song to the faster paced and more expressive worship. Everyone knew that the holiness church demonstrated the total opposite in worship; they were the trail blazers in use of different instrumentation, creating their own songs in the spirit, raising and clapping their hands, and dancing in the spirit. They were known for the faster paced songs of worship, where the Holy Spirit would fall and people would dance all around the church. The instruments would continue playing at an unbelievable rate, keeping up with the pace of the dancers in the congregation.

In 1930, Lizzie's local Bishop, V.M. Barker, started a traveling church band at his church, Barker Temple, in Kansas City, Missouri. I interviewed his oldest son, Victor Barker, on September 4, 1998; and his younger son, Flernoy Barker, on May 11, 1998. At this time he gave me a list of the individuals who played various instruments in his father's band. These are some of the church members in the 1930's and the instruments they played:

- Clifford Holt - Violin
- Brother Luke - Violin
- Brother Johnson - Trombone
- Victor Barker - Trombone
- Oscar Gibson - Horn
- Brother Reese - Bass Fiddle
- Pauline Richards - First church piano player
- Brother Kluke - wrote the song "Closer Walk With Thee"
- Mother Pickett - Drums

1945, Memphis, TN, Mother Lizzie Robinson's Last photo before she died in Memphis Convocation at year of Jubilee Celebration, L-R Bishop Riley F. Williams, Bishop O.T. Jones, SR, Bishop Roberts, Mother Lizzie Robinson and Mother Lillian Brooks-Coffey

- Ruth Baker - Tambourine

The Barker brothers stated that the band was popular in Kansas City because they were the first church band in their area. The other traditional churches looked upon playing instruments as a sin. The Barker brother's main theme for playing instruments was, "Let the Lord lead you." He described it in this way; a congregation member would start out singing, then the band would find out what key they were in and start playing. Most of the holiness churches would catch on by ear, in order to even keep up with the pace and style of music. He stated that people from the traditional churches would get out early from their services to come down to hear and watch the way the Barker Temple would worship God. The congregation would fall out under the power, sing, shout, play, and worship God with the evidence of speaking in other tongues.

Eventually this phenomena spread to other traditional Protestant denominations to the point that almost all Christian churches have segments that have adopted the worship styles of the Pentecostal and Holiness faiths.

Mother Robinson's Final Years and the Rebuilding of the National Temple

In 1936, eleven year after it had been built, the national temple at 958 S. 5th St. burned down. This was a tragic ending after all of the work that had been done to construct it in 1925. The national meetings were held at Bishop Mason's Church, located on 672 Lauderdale, from 1936 to 1945, when the present Mason Temple was constructed. Even through the main temple had burned; little did Mason realize that he would undertake building one of

Construction of Mason Temple, 1943, R-L Bishop A. B. McQwen, Bishop U. E. Miller, Elder J. O. Patterson

the largest facilities built at that time by an African-American. Mother Robinson diverted her fund-raising focus upon raising capitol to build the present Mason Temple. She was now seventy-six years old, and she had spent the majority of her life on the road laying the groundwork for the future of Mason's national denomination; and forging progressive reforms in the organization she loved so much.

In March of 1937, at seventy-seven years old, Mother Robinson experienced another setback. The Lord called her beloved husband and companion from labor to reward: Pastor Edward D. Robinson went home to be with the Lord.[20] Lizzie heard of his illness while she was on the road traveling from state to state raising money for the newly constructed temple in Memphis. She returned home after the convocation to attend to her husband's terminal illness. On his death certificate it was recorded that Lizzie was at home when Elder Robinson left this life to go from labor to reward. Her heart was heavy with grief that she would no long enjoy the companion that stood by her side for twenty-five years of marriage and ministry; a man who supported her travels and ministry efforts. Lizzie had to travel most of the year, but he stood by her dedication and love for God's Kingdom work. Dad Robinson had continued to pastor the local church the both of them founded twenty-one years earlier. He was a dedicated husband and Pastor that had became like a father to the main members in the church who called him Dad Robinson instead of Pastor. Bishop Mason came all the way to Omaha, Nebraska to perform Dad Robinson's eulogy at the first church they founded in the state of Nebraska. In a 1990 interview with Mother Lillian Chambers, one of the original charter members of the mother church in Nebraska, who was eighty years old during the

Lifted Banner Magazine for Women of the Churches of God in Christ, Mother Robinson started it in 1944, it lasted for thirty years

interview, stated that Bishop Mason came to perform the service for Dad Robinson. He wanted to give the utmost support to the two individuals that supported his national vision. A month following his death, Mother spent her seventy-seventh birthday alone without Dad Robinson. Nevertheless, although mother's grief was great, she said at the funeral, "*I cannot stop, I must work the work of him that sent me while it is day, for the night cometh and no man can work.*"

The time came when hard work and continued travel took its toll on Mother Robinson's weak frame. The last five years of her life she battled to regain her strength but she had to stay home directing her fund-raising program through her state mothers. Lizzie knew that her days were numbered, but she realized that she had to help to raise those finances to complete the current Mason temple construction project. One last project she implemented within the women's organization was to organize the Lifted Banner Magazine in 1944. This was completed a year before her death. This magazine became the official women's magazine for he women's ministry within the Churches of God in Christ. Published out of Mother's home, this magazine was one of the first African-American women's religious magazines in America. It remained in print for over thirty years after the death of Mother Lizzie Robinson.

When the Bible says she is far above rubies, Mother Robinson fits as a candidate. She was able to raise 1/3 of the $400.000 it took to build the present Mason Temple in Memphis, Tennessee. The year 1945, upon the completion of Mason Temple, was also the year of Jubilee celebration for Mason's organization. Mother Robinson wrote a letter to the church in celebration to the Year of Jubilee.

Mother Lillian Brooks-Coffey, secretary for Mother Lizzie for over 30 years became the next National Mother in 1946

Jubilee Celebration Letter from Mother Robinson

Date: 11-10-1945
Mother Lizzie Robinson
General Supervisor of Women's Work
2723 North 28th Avenue
Omaha, Nebraska

Bishop R.F. Williams national chairman Holy Greetings to you and the staff of Bishops at this writing I am glad to tell you how glad I am to live to see our Chief Apostle's Year of Jubilee in this great Church of God in Christ. When I read Leviticus 25:11 a Jubilee unto you and we are glad Bishop Williams. I am glad you and others have stood up. Exodus 17:12-13 Bishop needs now to hold up his hand in the twelfth verse they held his arms steady in the going down of the Sun, I am glad Bishop Williams I thank you and the staff of Bishops, overseers, pastors, state mothers and missionaries. I'm glad I can say I am one that is glad of the laity of this Great Church of God in Christ through this old hymn. Blow ye the trumpet. Blow the gladly sound let all the nations know that the year of Jubilee has come, the year of Jubilee return ye ransom sinners home. Ye slave of sin and shame your liberty obtains Redemption by his blood through all the earth proclaiming the year of Jubilee. I thank God that all the Bishops and Pastors all state Mothers and Missionaries are blessed with a great women auxiliary of the Church of God in Christ. Glad we do not have to go to other women's councils to settle our matters or other Brotherhoods to lead this church Bishop. I am asking this of you notice what I am sending to paper if I have made a mistake you correct it. My daughter says I call your name too much well you are the chairman of the Brother's Board, you are the speaker of the house, and you are next to Bishop Mason. Now blow the

Phone W. E. 3378

11 — 10 — 1945

Mother Lizzie Robinson
General Supervisor of Women's Work
2723 North 28th Avenue
OMAHA 10, NEBRASKA

Bishop R. E. Williams National Chairman Holy greeting
to you and the Staff of Bishops at this [illegible] I am
glad to tell you how glad I am to Live to See
our chief apostle. year of Jubilee in this
Church of God in Christ when Read Lev 25.11
a Jubilee unto you we are glad Bishop Williams great
glad you and other have stand up Exodus 17: 12—13. Bishop Read
[illegible] to hold up his hand [illegible] 12 [illegible] they hold his
[illegible] steady till the going of the I am glad Bishop
Williams I thank for you and the Staff Bishop and
and [illegible] State Mother and Missionary I glad [illegible]
Say I am [illegible] glad of the Unity of this great
Church of God in Christ think of this old hymn. Blow
ye the trumpet blow. the gladly solemn sound let all
the nations know to Earth remotest bound. the year
of Jubilee has come the year of Jubilee has come Return
ye ransomed Sinner home. ye Shame of Sin and Shame [illegible]
Liberty at [illegible] Redemption by his blood through
all the Earth proclaim. the year of Jubilee

Last Letter of Mother Lizzie, written by her own hand to the National Church, 1945

trumpets in Zion, shout aloud the Holy Command, let the Earth's inhabitants tremble for the Lord is at hand.[13]

YOURS MOTHER L. ROBINSON
11-10-1945

During the Year of Jubilee celebration, the state women's departments had grown. Mother Robinson started out experimenting with one Mother, Hannah Chandler, in the State of Texas in 1914. Now it was thirty-one years later, and she had built up a national network of women in ministry. It met with such success that every bishop in the brotherhood had a female leader at his side in the work for God's Kingdom, just as Bishop Mason had done with her on the national level. At her attendance of the Year of Jubilee celebration she had an official roll of forty-nine state mothers she had appointed to stand alongside different Bishops. This does not include the seven female missionaries that she funded to build schools, churches, clients, dormitories, and orphanages in Africa, the West Indies, and the pacific islands. Here is the list of the host of women she developed into Deborah's' to lay a groundwork for future females to build upon for years to come.

STATE MOTHERS OFFICIAL ROLL, December 1945

- Mother Lizzie Robinson, General Supervisor of Women Work, 2723 N. 28th Ave, Omaha, Nebraska
- Mother Lillian Brooks-Coffey, Assistant General Supervisor of Women Work, State Mother of S.W. Michigan, Ohio and Georgia, 429 E. 44th St., Chicago, Illinois.

Women of the National Church over the years

- Mother Adair Addie, W. Tennessee, 220 Reno Ave., Memphis, Tennessee.
- Mother Anderson, F.M., North Carolina, 300 Hood St., Rockingham, North Carolina.
- Mother Bailey, Annie L., Maryland, Delaware, D.C. and New Jersey, 4629 Vinewood Ave., Detroit, Michigan.
- Mother Beck, Fannie, North Mississippi, P.O. Box 141, Tutwiler, Mississippi.
- Mother Benson, Emma, Iowa, 2607 Decator St. Omaha, Nebraska.
- Mother Boone, Tena, W. Missouri and Nebraska, 1143 N. Senate Ave. Indianapolis, Ind.
- Mother Bostic, Lucendia, E. Missouri, 3115 Vine Grove St., St, Louis, MO.
- Mother Buchanan, c., S. Mississippi, 2604 Indiana Ave., apt. 3, Chicago, Illinois.
- Mother Broadnax, Hannah, E. Tennessee, 112 Silverage Ave., Memphis, Tenn.
- Mother Bufkins, Bobbie, Minnesota, 2318 N. 27th Ave., Omaha, Nebraska.
- Mother Byars, Mattie, Kansas, 1241 State Ave., Kansas City, Kansas.
- Mother Chambers, Emma, Wisconsin, 2505 Corby St. Omaha, Nebraska.
- Mother Dabney, Beulah L., Virginia 125 Richardson St. Staunton, Virginia.
- Mother Davis, Mary, N., Illinois, 1342 W. 111th St., Chicago, Illinois.
- Mother Douglas, Ritta, Washington, 1807 Grass St., Spokane, Washington.
- Mother Drake, Sarah, South Carolina, 18 F. St., Charleston, South Carolina.

Women of the National Church over the years

- Mother Ford, Jessie, N. Dakota. 225 e. 31st St. Chicago, Illinois.

- Mother Gamble, Nancy, So. Illinois and Indiana, 3590 Penn, Ave., E. Chicago, Indiana.
- Mother Graham, A.P., Montana, 423 S. 25th St., Billings, Montana.
- Mother Hale, L.O. Southern California, 1376 E. 111th St., Los Angeles, Calif.
- Mother Henderson, Lula, Western Florida 342 Park St., Jacksonville, Florida.
- Mother Henderson, C.A., Arizona, 1329 E. Adams, Phoenix, Arizona.
- Mother Hollis, Eliza, Louisiana, Route 6, Box 121, Pine Bluff, Arkansas.
- Mother Hutson, M.E., Vermont, 2748 Franklin St., Denver, Colorado.
  - Mother Holt, Willie, Idaho, 1140 Elmore St., Idaho Falls, Idaho.
  - Mother Johnson, Mary, Northeast Michigan and Canada, 227 E. Palmer St., Detroit, Michigan.
  - Mother Jones, E.L. Colorado, 2121 Marion St., Denver, Colorado.
  - Mother Johnson, Joan, New Mexico, 110 Rencher St., Colvis, New Mexico.
  - Mother Jennings, Alberta, Utah, 244 Poplar St., Salt Lake City, Utah.
  - Mother Key, Manior, Alabama, 1031 N. 4th, Birmingham 4, Alabama.
  - Mother Lindsay, Rosia, Arkansas, Route 4, Box 743, Pine Bluff, Arkansas.
  - Mother Logan, Amy, New Hampshire, 20 Raymond St. S., Norwalk, Connecticut.
  - Mother Martin, Mable, Rhode Island, 128B Point St. Providence 3, R.I.
  - Mother Matthews, D.M. Connecticut, 89 Canton St., Hartford, Connect

- Mother Metcalf, S. L., Kentucky, 705 Hopewell St., Maisonville, Kentucky.
- Mother McGlothen, M., Northern California, 1444 Kelsy St., Richmond, Calif.
- Mother Miller, Lee, Oregon, 1633 Alcatraz Ave., Berkeley, California.
- Mother Mayse, Beulah, Nevada, 1259 Webster St., San Francisco, California.
- Mother Patterson, Hattie, Wyoming, 804 S.W. Front St., Rawlins 3, Wyoming.
- Mother Payton, Madye, New York, 415 Madison St., Syracuse, New York.
- Mother Polk, Bertha, Texas, Box 425 (P.O. Box). Childress, Texas.
- Mother Riley, Della, Eastern Florida, 561 Loomis Ave., Daytona Beach, Florida.
- Mother Ways H.M., Pennsylvania, 5535 Wyalusing Ave., Philadelphia, Pennsylvania.
- Mother Washington, Jesse, West Virginia, 409 E. Grand Ave., Hot Springs, Ark.
- Mother Wheeler, Fannie, South Dakota, 1337 N. Main St., Sioux Falls, South Dakota.
- Mother Williams, Lula, Oklahoma, Box 3, Muldrow, Oklahoma. [21]

Mother Robinson's Funeral in Omaha, NE. 1945

Mother Robinson Head stone purchase by COGIC

As Mother realized that this would be her last convocation, she wanted to see the new temple constructed. Mother felt she had finished her course and that she would not return home. She had to attend this last important convocation and the dedication of the new Mason Temple, which, with a seating capacity of 8,000, was at that time the largest facility that an African-American organization had built. She took her journey southward to visit this newly completed edifice. Lizzie, at the age of eight-four, seemed to take on new strength as she walked through the building examining it for soundness, looking at the work of her hands, and sitting in the assembly hall which bore her name. She held the final conference with her state mothers throughout the United States that attended the convocation, reviewing the constitution of the women's work of the church.

Mother realized that one thing she desired for the building was missing, and that was a sign in front of the national temple. Mother asked her daughter Ida to take her personal money and purchase a large neon sign for the front of Mason Temple, which still stands there today, reading, National Headquarters of the Churches of God in Christ. She went to her room tired and weary and in a few hours drew the drapery of her couch about her and fell asleep in Jesus. This ended the career of one of the greatest organizers among Christian women.

This was a sad time all over the Church of God in Christ denomination, because her life had touched so many other lives during the course of her life. Since she died at the convocation, two funerals were celebrated, one in Memphis, TN where Bishop C.H. Mason eulogized her. Then her body was shipped back to her hometown of Omaha, Nebraska where the mother church mourned her, and Bishop O.T.

Jones eulogized her for the local church family. Mother Dollie Matthews gave Mother Robinson a gift from the Women's Department. It was a dress with pearl buttons down the front. Mother Robinson really liked it, and during her final convocation she wore the dress. At her death, her daughter Ida buried her in that dress she loved so well. She was buried in the Mt. Hope Cemetery in Omaha, Nebraska. Her headstone reads, "Mother Lizzie Robinson, National Supervisor of the Women's Work Department of the Churches of God in Christ."

Chapter 7

Epilogue—The 1990 Renaissance & Preservation of Mother Robinson's History

It was in 1990 that the Lord began to deal with me surrounding the pioneers of the twentieth-century Pentecostal Movement. Bishop McDaniel had just passed, and the national Church of God in Christ was deciding on who would be selected as the next Bishop of the Church of God in Christ in Nebraska. Several pastors were in the running for the position, so Presiding Bishop L.H. Ford appointed Bishop P.A. Brooks of Michigan to be interim Bishop until the decision was finalized. Bishop Vernon Richardson, the pastor of Faith Temple C.OG.I.C., he was the eldest candidate and had served as a pastor the longest in Nebraska.

I pastored my own church at the time. I had been praying about the next leadership for the jurisdiction, when God showed me that pastor Richardson would be the next Bishop of Nebraska. Many of the younger men did not want Pastor Richardson to be Bishop; they wanted a younger man to take the position. I went over to pastor Richardson's house that weekend, and I told him that God showed me that the national church would select him as the next bishop of Nebraska. He stated to me, "Are you sure son." I told him, standing in his living room, that I knew for a surety it would happen just as God had shown me.

It was six months later that the international presiding Bishop, L.H. Ford, returned back to Nebraska to select from a pool of eight people a bishop for Nebraska. In September of 1991, Pastor Vernon Richardson was selected as the next Bishop of Nebraska. Bishop Richardson asked me what I wanted to do in the jurisdiction, and I asked him to allow me to be the historian for the state of Nebraska. He gave me the appointment three months later after his first jurisdictional organizational meeting. I was humbled that the Lord allowed me to tell Bishop Richardson what God had in store for his future.

Following that incident, I entered into several days of fasting and had a vision that the Late Bishop C.H. Mason and Mother Lizzie Robinson were telling me to research their history and make sure that the younger generations knew about the foundation they laid in the church. It surprised me, when I awoke from the vision I thought, "How could I have had this conversation with these two pioneers who had passed away forty to fifty years ago?" Nevertheless, I knew that it was God that had allowed me to see what I saw. I was instructed to research the contributions of the woman that worked alongside the founder, Bishop C.H. Mason. As I began my research, I discovered she lived in Omaha, Nebraska for most of her tenure as the first international supervisor of women for the Church of God in Christ. [22]

Omaha Press Conference Presiding Bishop Ford in Omaha 1991

Presiding Bishop L.H. Ford talks to Omaha community about How Omaha is significant to the National Church's future

Bishop Urges Church of God in Christ to Return to Roots

Rudy Smith, World-Herald

Ford . . . "The Church of God in Christ has always been a church that believed in economic development."

By Julia McCord
World-Herald Staff Writer

The presiding bishop of the Church of God in Christ on Friday called on the church to go back to its roots in order to secure the future.

At a press conference at the Red Lion Inn, the Rev. Louis H. Ford of Chicago said Omaha is a key player in the effort.

"Omaha can do more to bring us back to where we want to go than any other city in America," Ford said. "That's because the (church's) roots are so deeply planted and woven together here."

Omaha was home to Lizzie Robinson, who Ford said was one of the church's "pioneering ladies."

In 1906 Mrs. Robinson helped the denomination's founder, Bishop Charles H. Mason, organize and structure the church. She was the first supervisor of women's auxiliaries.

From modest beginnings in Lexington, Miss., the Church of God in Christ has grown to 3.7 million members in 22 countries. But it has forgotten its tradi-

66 OMAHA WORLD-HERALD Saturday, September 21, 198[illegible]

tional constituency, the disenfranchised, Ford said.

"What did our church specialize in back then?" he asked. "Grass-roots people."

The church preaches a mix of pentacostalism and entrepreneurship, training its converts in the ways of business as well as in the ways of God.

"The Church of God in Christ has always been a church that believed in economic development," Ford said. "The church works from the top down (God) and from the bottom up (business)."

During the Great Depression, for example, the church taught people to farm, to sew, to run businesses. In Memphis, a black-owned bank financed farmers and other entrepreneurs when times got tough.

Today, Ford said, the church needs "to be the example for returning back to the roots of the real black church of America that lives for the people, by the people."

"We're going to stop turning our heads on the dope addicts, the prostitutes," he said. With a "little bit more love, a little bit more care," 90 percent can be brought to Christ, he said.

The church needs to open child care centers all across America, halfway houses and shelters in every large city, and "get boys and girls to (the farm) to make them see livestock, let them plant fruit trees, teach them to be builders."

"Let's open some stores, stop marching and put the money to working," he

Please turn to Page 66, Col. 1

Ford came to Omaha for the 74th Annual Holy Convocation of the Nebraska Jurisdiction, which concludes today.

The northeast and eastern Nebraska jurisdictions recently merged because of the death of one bishop and the illness of another.

Ford said he had come to bring about unity "and begin the real growth with this state."

Bishop P.S. Brooks from Detroit was appointed interim bishop of the newly created jurisdiction in December and will serve until a permanent bishop can be named.

Bishop Says Omaha Key To His Church

● Continued from Page 65

said. "That's what our church is all about."

In the spiritual arena, Ford said, the church also needs to get down to business. It needs to carry Jesus' message of salvation out into the streets.

"We still believe in all-night prayer, asking, praying, clapping our hands and stomping our hands and screaming," he said. "We will not run from our responsibilities in the community."

Bishop Urges Church of God in Christ to Return to Roots, and Bishop Says Omaha Key To His Church
By Julia McCord Omaha World-Herald Staff Writer. Saturday September 21, 1991

The presiding bishop of the Church of God in Christ on Friday called on the church to go back to its roots in order to secure the future. At a press conference at the Red Lion Inn, the Rev. Louis H. Ford of Chicago said Omaha is a key player in the effort. "Omaha can do more to bring us back to where we want to go than any other city in America," Ford said. "That's because the (church's) roots are so deeply planted and woven together here." Omaha was home to Lizzie Robinson, who Ford said was on of the church's "pioneering ladies."

In 1906 Mrs. Robinson helped the denomination's founder, Bishop Charles H. Mason, organize and structure the church. She was the first supervisor of women's auxiliaries. From modest beginnings in Lexington, MS, the Church of God in Christ has grown to 3.7 million members in 52 countries. But it has forgotten its traditional constituency, the disenfranchised, Ford said. "What did our church specialize in back then? He asked. "Grass-roots people." The church preaches a mix of Pentecostalism and entrepreneurship, training its converts in the ways of business as well as in the ways of God.

"The Church of God in Christ has always been a church that believed in economic development," Ford said. "The church works from the top down (God) and from the bottom up (business). During the Great Depression, for example, the church taught people to farm, to sew, to run businesses. In Memphis, a black-owned bank financed farmers and other entrepreneurs when times got tough.

Today, Ford said the church needs "to be the example for returning back to the roots of the real black church of America that lives for the people, by the people." We're going to stop turning our heads on the dope addicts, the prostitutes, "he said. With a "little bit more love, a little bit more care." 90 percent can be brought to Christ, he said.

The church needs to open child care centers all across America, halfway houses and shelters in every large city, and "get boys and girls to (the farm) to make them see livestock, let them plant fruit trees, teach them to be builders." Let's open some stores, stop marching and put the money to working," he said. "That's what our church is all about.

In the spiritual arena, Ford said, the church also needs to get down to business. It needs to carry Jesus message of salvation out into the streets. "We still believe in all-night prayer, fasting, praying, clapping our hands and stomping our feet and screaming, " he said. "We will not run from our responsibilities in the community."

The next event that took place was when we came up before the city board to review whether the mother church of

Nebraska was significant of being recognized by civic authorities as a historic landmark. The church that was named after her and her husband was selected to be a historical site by the city board because of Mother Robinson's historic and international significance. I submitted the information to Bishop Richardson, and then told him that we needed to get the national church involved. I wrote another article to go in the Whole Truth Paper about the civic authorities recognizing Mother Lizzie Robinson's church as a historic landmark. The article was published in the worldwide Whole Truth Newspaper.

The city planning department helped me organize my argument to the Federal Registry of Historic places to request their recognition of Mother Lizzie Robinson as a significant figure in the history of America. It took about six to eight months following our preparation of the nomination application. After its preparation I had to travel to Lincoln, Nebraska to convince the State Historical Society to vote to allow the nomination to proceed to Washington, D.C.

The property that Mother Robinson used to own as her home was currently owned by the city, as they had taken it for taxes not paid after her death. The city told me that the interstate came through that area, her lot was adjacent to the Highway and that the city owned easement rights on the lot. The only way the property could be taken back was to pay the back taxes, and request that the city planning department release the property for historic reasons. I finally persuaded the city-planning department to release the lot. We did not have any money in the historic committee, since we had just started the jurisdiction. Therefore, I purchased the lot through

Letter From Faith Temple Church of God in Christ From State Historian Elder Elijah L. Hill, December 16, 1991

December 16, 1991

Church of God in Christ
Presiding Bishop's Office
272 S. Main St.
Memphis, TN. 38103

Dear Honorable Presiding Bishop L. H. Ford

At the desire of our State Bishop and his vision to restore the State of Nebraska to a point whereby the National work can be proud of our historical significance that relates to her glory.

Bishop Vernon Richardson has installed me as the State Historian for C.O.G.I.C for the State of Nebraska. We would like to accomplish those things that would enhance the historical knowledge of the people that live here in our State of Nebraska. For we have been greatly encouraged and moved by your desire to see those things of the past restored and honored for they are the foundation upon which our beginnings lie.

When you were here in Omaha at the Press Conference you spoke so profoundly concerning the historical significance of Omaha, Nebraska, in relationship to Mother Lizzie Robinson, who was the first General

Mother while the National Church was in her infancy stage.

The Bishop and I, feel that you have stirred up the gift that is within us to let it be known to the residents of our great city of Omaha, Nebraska., by way of us requesting that there be a written Proclamation from the National Church confirming; that Omaha, Nebraska, is of historical meaning to the Mother Church in Memphis, TN.

Enclosed, is an example of what I have researched to be true and correct information that could be included in the official document, which we understand that the final acceptance of the wording will rest upon the Presiding Bishop's final approval and wishes.

Yours That His Kingdom Will Come

Bishop Vernon Richardson

Pastor Elijah L. Hill
State Historian for the State of Nebraska

Letter From Faith Temple Church of God in Christ From State Historian Elder Elijah L. Hill, January 28, 1992

January 28, 1992

International Supervisor
Dr. Mattie McGlothen
412 Sanford Avenue
Richmond, CA 94801

Dear Dr. McGlothen

As per our telephone conversation the morning of January 28, 1992 around 9:00am. I made mention to you about our State Historical Department's desire to have a letter of support form the Women's Convention. Concerning an application filed with the City of Omaha's Landmark Heritage Preservation Commission.

There will be a public hearing on February 12, 1992 at 1:30pm at the downtown Omaha Civic Center to consider nomination of two properties that are of historical value to Mother Lizzie Robinson, when she was alive. Enclosed along with this letter is a public notice of the hearing, if you could provide us with a letter of support before the hearing date. I am sure it will strengthen our State Bishop's position at the hearing. Send your correspondence to myself, Pastor Elijah L. Hill, P.O. Box 11550, Omaha, Nebraska. 68111.

Yours that His Kingdom Will Come

Pastor Elijah L. Hill, Th. B
State Historian of the Churches of God
in Christ in Nebraska

CC: Presiding Bishop L. H. Ford
Bishop Vernon Richardson

At this time the presiding Bishop L.H. Ford was reviving the history of the late founder bishop C.H. Mason. He had, in 1955, gotten a street named after Bishop Mason. He had a national committee formed to research the history of the earlier pioneers of the Church of God in Christ. His main focus was on the founder Bishop C.H. Mason, while the Lord told me to work on the history of Mother Robinson. Her history could be easily researched, since she lived in Omaha, Nebraska where I lived at the time. My instructions in prayer were to do everything for Mother Robinson that the national church was doing for the founder, Bishop Mason.

Therefore, I came up with a plan to accomplish four things in the area of history for Nebraska:

1. To have a street named after Mother Robinson.
2. To have the first church started by her and her husband protected as a historic landmark.
3. To write a nomination for the last existing home of her daughter, placed on the Federal Registry of historic places.
4. To purchase the land where Mother Robinson's home used to exist, and build a Museum on it.

A meeting was arranged at Bishop Richardson's house where the bishop and I talked about my plans for the history of Nebraska. Bishop Richardson was surprised that I had such a great vision, when he had just appointed me as the historian. I told Bishop Richardson that God wanted me to accomplish these things during his administration because God wanted him to be recognized by the national church. I told him some of the ministers thought that if they could sit on him because of his age, they would wear him down, so one day they could take his place. I told him that God had a plan, at his then age of eight-two, to bless him more in his latter days and to be recognized for the chosen vessel he was. I told Bishop the only thing I asked was that when all this success began to occur that he would back me up with the pastors, because I believed they would try to come between us to stop what God was doing. Bishop Richardson told me he appreciated the plan that God had given me, and that he wanted to pray for me that God would give me the ability to do all that I had in my heart.

I wrote a letter to presiding Bishop L.H. Ford, a letter signed by Bishop Richardson, outlining the fact that we wanted to research the historic roots of the Church of God in Christ in Nebraska, and do whatever we could to bring about a renaissance of C.O.G.I.C. history back in our state. I told Bishop that it was important that the national church be aware of what our intentions were, so that as things materialized they would give us their support.

After I researched Mother Robinson's history in detail for six months, I was reading the Whole Truth

World Headquarters
Memphis, Tennessee USA

Office of the Presiding Bishop

Proclamation

Whereas: Our Late Founder, Bishop Charles Harrison Mason, envisioned the magnitude of including the women of THE CHURCH OF GOD IN CHRIST, INC., that they were in need of organization and direction while the National Church was in its stage of infancy, and;

Whereas: Our Late Mother Lizzie Robinson was appointed as the First General Supervisor of Women of THE CHURCH OF GOD IN CHRIST by our Founder, Bishop Charles Harrison Mason, in and around 1911, and;

Whereas: Due to the rapid growth of the Church and Mother Robinson's God-given skills in organizing, she gave great direction and support to the National Women's Work, by creating auxiliaries such as the Bible Band, Sewing Circle, Home and Foreign Mission, Sunshine Band, Purity Class, State Mothers Unit, and Secretaries Unit. Also, she prayerfully selected and appointed a hose of choice women, many of whom were sent to different States in the United States to be helpers to the Overseers (Bishops) that were appointed by our Founding Father, and;

Whereas: Mother Robinson hailed from the great City of Omaha, Nebraska, and she resided there until the date she was promoted to glory in the month of December 1945 while attending the National Convocation in Memphis, Tennessee, and;

Be It Therefore Resolved:

Bishop Vernon Richardson has appointed a State Historian in the State of Nebraska in order to research and verify that which will enhance the history of the CHURCH OF GOD IN CHRIST in the State of Nebraska under the auspices of Elder Elijah Hill and by the will of the CHURCH OF GOD CHRIST there in Omaha, Nebraska;

Be It Finally Resolved:

That the eight day of July in this year of our Lord, one thousand nine hundred and ninety-two be a DAY OF MEMORIAL to honor the life and work of Mother Lizzie Robinson, the First National Supervisor who has fallen asleep in Jesus.

Given under my hand and the Seal of the Presiding Bishop at the World Headquarters in the City of Memphis, Tennessee, this 27th day of March in the year of our Lord one thousand nine hundred and ninety two.

L. H. Ford

Presiding Bishop

Newspaper, and I decided to take the history I researched and request a proclamation from the national church to validate the history. Bishop gave me the permission to contact the national church. The presiding Bishop's office gladly received the historic information about Mother Lizzie Robinson, and six months later sent us back an official proclamation. I told Bishop that we had something from the church; in order to make sure no one else purchased it when it came up for sale.

This proclamation was a way the national church was validating her history, so that when I approached the civic officials, our official document would validate their support. Next, I called the city of Omaha's planning department to find out what the criteria was to change a street name. Then I called the city of Omaha's Historical Landmark Board to find out their qualifications for a property to be placed under their protection as a historic landmark. Needless to say I was given the run around many times, but I stayed persistent. If one department held me up with their answer, I would call about my other project. I kept following up with all four projects until progress was made on each one.

Once progress was made, I met again with Bishop Richardson, and explained all the details to him to get his input. The national church delayed the proclamation, so I asked Bishop Richardson if he would allow me to speak as his spokesperson to the presiding Bishop about our request, in the capacity as the historian for Bishop's jurisdiction. I called the presiding Bishop's office in Chicago, and I spoke with Presiding Bishop L.H. Ford that next morning. I explained that we were looking into getting a street named after Mother Robinson to uphold the historic strides he was making with the history of Bishop C.H. Mason. The presiding Bishop assured me that he would have his secretary in Memphis, Tennessee send us the document. He also was having his historical committee make sure that the national church validated all of the information I had submitted.

I wrote the national Whole Truth Newspaper of the Church of God in Christ about receiving the proclamation, and shared with them that the Mayor of Omaha also recognized the worldwide works of Mother Robinson as important to Omaha. Eventually, an article was published

The Whole Truth News Paper
March 1993

On February 27, 1993, Bishop Vernon Richardson prelate of Nebraska and Elder Elijah L. Hill received the Governor's Recognition Award form Governor E. Benjamin Nelson. The award was presented to Bishop Vernon Richardson for his willingness and insight to appoint a historian to establish the rich Nebraska history of the Church of God in Christ. Elder Elijah L. Hill was sighted for his civic achievement towards the renaissance and preservation of Mother Lizzie Robinson's history in the state of Nebraska. The night of the occasion Governor E. Benjamin had someone to read a personalized letter to Elder Hill, stating that, "This effort speaks well of your dedication to both the State and the Church and you are most deserving of this award." The International Chairman of the General

Assembly, Dr. Frank Ellis, was present at the Red Lion Hotel, Ball Room, in Omaha, Nebraska.

Elder Elijah L. Hill has also appeared before the State of Nebraska's Historical Society, on January 8, 1993, in Lincoln, NE., accompanied by Lynn Meyer of the City of Omaha's City Planning department. Lynn Meyer is the City of Omaha's Historic Preservation Administrator, who supported Elder Hill's nomination of Ida Baker's former home that is seventy-nine years old. Elder Hill made a fifteen minutes slide presentation to the Historical Society's Board, then they voted unanimously to nominate the last home that was significant in association with the First General Mother Lizzie Robinson, a historic site. Mother Robinson's former residence was condemned in 1975. Elder Robert Alexander presently lives in Ida's Baker's house, who is her foster son. He states that many of the old pioneers would come through, and visit during the time that Mother Lizzie Robinson was alive because of her national position as general mother. During Bishop C.H. Mason's travels through other states in the Midwest, he stopped through to personally talk with Mother Lizzie Robinson.

Mother Robinson's actual home was smaller than Ida's home, commonly referred to as the "big house." Bishop C.H. Mason would stay at Ida Bakers home and many other of the old pioneers like; Mother Lillian Brooks-Coffey. Bishop Mason preached the funeral of Mother Lizzie Robinson, since she died while at the Memphis Convocation. Mother Dollie M. Matthews, the third state mother of Connecticut presented the last gift from he national women's department. She presented to Mother Robinson a beautiful white satin, princess style dress with pretty buttons down the front. At Mother Robinson's last annual national women's day in Memphis, Tenn., 1945. Mother wore her dress. Her daughter, Ida Baker, "Big Sister" she was called, laid her to rest in it. Mother Lillian Brooks-Coffey made sure that everything was in order in finalizing her burial in Omaha in December 1945. She purchased a beautiful granite head stone that reads, "Mother Lizzie Robinson the First General Supervisor of the Women's Department of the Church of God in Christ," she was buried at the Mt Hope Cemetery in Omaha, Nebraska.

"The Lifted Banner," a magazine established in 1944 by the National Women's Department, was printed and circulated out of Mother Robinson's former home. The magazine continued for over thirty or more years before it went out of print. We thank Mother Robinson for her untiring love for the growth of the international organization. Before Mother Robinson died, she had the present neon sign at International Headquarters installed December 1945. Mother Mattie McGlothen had the replica of the Omaha street sign, named after Mother Lizzie Robinson, and allowed Elder Hill space to present it during Women's Day at the 85th Holy Convocation. Mother Mattie McGlothen is one of the last original state mother's who was appointed by the Late First General Mother Lizzie Robinson.

Reported

Elder Elijah L. Hill
A Way Out of No Way COGIC

1992 Elder Hill and Bishop Vernon Richardson at Governor's Mansion

1991 L-R Bishop Sanders, Presiding Bishop Ford, and Elder Elijah Hill

about these two proclamations in the Whole Truth Newspaper. Bishop was really pleased with how God was blessing me to prosper in all the things I was putting my hands to do.

I knew that the city council would give me problems with the street name change. The city planning director told me, "Rev. Hill, you are setting a precedence; we have never given a street name change to a female, white or black." He assured me that I could attempt it, but that he would not support it when it went to city council. I knew that one angle they would come up with was that the residents that lived along that three block stretch would not want it changed. Therefore, I researched all the owners, wrote up a petition and asked them if they would support me by signing the petition when I met with the city council.

The Lord blessed me to get all of the owners on both sides of the street to sign the petition, after explaining to them the purpose of the street name was for a historically significant individual to be recognized for their accomplishments. I began to research how we could bring the women's convention to Omaha, Nebraska. The convention and visitors bureau of the city of Omaha did an analysis on the women's convention. They told me that the women's convention was 30,000 or more attendees, and that it was too large for the city of Omaha to host. They told me that they did not know of many conventions they had dealt with that were that big.

The analysis from the convention and visitors bureau demonstrated the millions of dollars that would impact the business community if they came here for a week. I asked her to write a letter to the president of the city council, Joe

Mrs. Robinson and her husband, Edward, started the first Nebraska congregation in Omaha in 1916. Both are deceased.

That was 10 years after she helped Bishop Charles Harrison Mason found the church in Lexington, Miss.

Erskine Street from 24th to 27th Streets will be renamed in honor of Mrs. Robinson. Among the supporters of the change were Pastor Elijah L. Hill, state historian for the church.

The predominantly black Church of God in Christ has 3.7 million members worldwide and is the second largest black church in the United States. The church has 16 congregations in Nebraska, including 13 in Omaha.

Robinson Memorial Church, 2318 N. 26th St., is named after the Robinsons. In June, the council designated the church and the former Robinson residence at 2864 Corby St. as historic landmarks. The designations were approved in February by the Landmarks Heritage Preservation Commission.

Omaha World-Herald
Wednesday, August 5, 1992 15

Council Says: Here's to You, Mrs. Robinson

BY JOE BRENNAN
WORLD-HERALD STAFF WRITER

Omaha's newest street name is Lizzie Robinson Avenue.

The City Council voted Tuesday to rename a three-block stretch of Erskine Street for the woman who helped organize the Church of God in Christ in Nebraska. The council approved the ordinance unanimously.

■ Tax increases and job cuts draw fire at Omaha budget hearing. Page 23.
■ Lottery and sales-tax money will help LaVista double its budget. Page 17.

"Lizzie Robinson is significant historically for her role as organizer of the women's ministry for the church," said City Planning Director Gary Pryor.

Omaha's Largest Newspaper Announces the City Council gives their first street naming for Mother Lizzie Robinson, 1992

Friend, allowing him to see that the importance of Mother Lizzie Robinson having this type of recognition would be to the city economic advantage. The city councilman told me that he had seen the work that I had done for the street name, and that he would make sure at that night of the hearing we would have the necessary votes to get the street name passed.

Many thought that I would not be able to accomplish the street change. Some of the older people wondered how I could know more about Mother Robinson, when I was not even born before she died. Nevertheless, God had blessed me with the necessary know-how to research her information in detail. During research, I traveled to Memphis, TN, and located every document I could that talked about Mother Lizzie Robinson. Some of the documents that I pulled included:

1. Her last will and testament
2. The deed of her home she purchased.
3. Her deed of record of the mother church.
4. The deed of record of Ida Baker's home.
5. I traced her daughter by finding her name in the cross-city directory from 1912 to 1925.

Piece by piece like a puzzle I was able to fit together the pattern of history of this great humanitarian.

Bishop L.H. Ford was about to be up for reelection as presiding bishop. I had submitted a resolution to the National Church's General Assembly to approve a one-day holiday for the first general mother to be recognized by the national church. The resolution was not allowed to go to the General Assembly. I got word that it needed to go past the presiding bishop before it went to the General Assembly. Bishop L.H.

Council Says: Here's to You, Mrs. Robinson Omaha World-Herald Wednesday, August 5, 1992

Joe Brennan Staff-writer

Omaha's newest street name is Lizzie Robinson Avenue. The City Council voted Tuesday to rename a three-block stretch of Erskine Street for the woman who helped organize the Church of God in Christ in Nebraska. The council approved the ordinance unanimously. "Lizzie Robinson is significant historically for her role as organizer of the women's ministry for the church," said City Planning Director Gary Pryor.

Mrs. Robinson and her husband, Edward started the first Nebraska congregation in Omaha in 1916. Both are deceased. That was 10 years after she helped Bishop Charles Harrison Mason found the church in Lexington, MS. Erskine Street from 24th to 27th Streets will be renamed in honor of Mrs. Robinson. Among the supporters of the change was Pastor Elijah L. Hill, state historian for the church.

The predominantly black Church of God in Christ has 3.7 million members worldwide and is the second largest black church in the United States. The church has 16 congregations in Nebraska including 13 in Omaha.

Robinson Memorial Church, 2318 N. 26th St., is named after the Robinsons. In June, the council designated the church and the former Robinson residence at 2864 Corby St. as historic landmarks. The designations were approved in February by the Landmarks Heritage Preservation Commission.

Ford asked my Bishop, Vernon Richardson, to speak on Saturday at the International Holy Convocation. He told me he had never had this kind of an opportunity in all his sixty years of preaching in the Churches of God in Christ. I told Bishop Richardson this was what God was showing me when I first started two years prior; that he would be blessed beyond his expectation when it came to being recognized by the national church.

I took Bishop Richardson to Lincoln, Nebraska with me to introduce him to Governor Ben Nelson. He told me, "Son you going to take me to meet the governor of Nebraska?" I told him the governor was going to give me an award for bringing about a renaissance of the history of Mother Lizzie Robinson. This would be a good time for him to take a picture with the governor that we could send to the Church's Whole Truth Newspaper. This would show the national church that we were being progressive on getting the secular world to acknowledge the history of the Church of God in Christ.

Elder Robert Alexander, who was the foster son of Ida Baker, Mother Lizzie Robinson's only daughter, gave me a lot of information about Mother Robinson, and how the national church worked. I interviewed several individuals to match together the consistence of the testimony. Individuals I interviewed for this book, over fourteen years of research, Included: Bishop B.T. McDaniel, Mother Lillian Chambers, Mother McDaniels, Bishop Vernon Richardson, Sister Naomi V. Lewis, Mother Franklin, Flenroy Barker, Victor Barker, Evalon Jones, Elise B. Moore, Virginia Lee, Elder Alonzo J.

Wright, Elder Robert M. Alexander, Mother Beatrice Watkins, Geneva Holt and Elder Alphonzo Bell.

The Whole Truth News Paper October 1992

IT'S OFFICIAL NOW

The Omaha City Council voted to renamed a three-block stretch of Erskine Street from 24th to 27th to Lizzie Robinson Avenue, in honor of the woman who helped organize the Women's Department for the Church of God in Christ International, which is the second largest black Church in the United States. Pastor Elijah Hill, State Historian for the Nebraska Church of God in Christ, served as the driving force to obtain the recognition for one of the true pioneering ladies of the Church of God in Christ International.

The official Lizzie Robinson street sign was installed Friday morning, August 21, 1992, in Omaha, by a City of Omaha Public Works employee. Several people were present to observe the historic event of the street installation of Lizzie Robinson Avenue. She was the first African-American female to receive this honor in Omaha, Nebraska. Among those present was (L-R): State Historian and Mrs. Elijah Hill, State Supervisor Louise Secreat and Bishop Vernon Richardson.

In February of this year, Elder Hill obtained the historic landmark designation for Robinson Memorial Church of God in Christ, 2318 N. 26th St., which was founded by

Mr. Edward and Lizzie Robinson. The church is presently named after the Robinson's. The former residence at 2864 Corby Street also was named as a Historic landmark in Omaha.

Mayor P. J. Morgan of the City of Omaha, in the month of September 1992, has recommended the State Historian Elder Elijah Hill, to be appointed to the City of Omaha's Landmark Heritage Preservation Commission. Under the leadership of Elder Hill, the Nebraska Historic Committee is seeking to obtain some other land that was owned my Mother Lizzie Robinson to re-landscape and rebuild a religious and historic library in her honor.

Elder Hill has also requested that Omaha's City Planning Department submit for nomination the last extant house that is associated with Mother Lizzie Robinson, to be forwarded to the Federal Registry of National Historic Places.

Omaha World-Hera
★ Friday, August 21, 1992

Stretch of Erskine Now Lizzie Robinson Avenue

It is now official. A three-block stretch of Erskine Street, from 24th to 27th, also will be known as Lizzie Robinson Avenue. The street name recognizes the woman who helped organize the Church of God in Christ in Nebraska in 1916. The church has 16 congregations in Nebraska, including 13 in Omaha. Robinson Memorial Church at 2318 N. 26th St. is named for Mrs. Robinson and her husband, Edward. Both are deceased. Ennis Lipscomb, a City of Omaha employee, is pictured installing the new sign Friday morning.

Mother Robinson Street Installation, 1992

Works Cited

---

[4] . Division of Vital Statistics City of Omaha, NE. Certificate of Death, Lizzie Robinson. Douglas, County. December 1945.
[5] Courts, James, Prof. The History and Life Work of Bishop C.H. Mason. Reprinted in 1924. Page 112,113
[1]In Christ Stead Autobiographical sketch. By Joanna P. Moore. Chicago, Illinois; Published by The Women's Baptist Home Mission Society, Indiana.
[2] Ibid
[3] Ibid
[1] Ibid
[1] Ibid
[1] Ibid
[5] Ibid
[7] Pleas, Charles H. Fifty Years Achievement From 1906-1956: A Period of the Church of God in Christ. Page 12-15.
[7] Ibid
[8] Burgess, Stanley M., and McGee, Gary B., Eds. Dictionary of Pentecostal and Charismatic Movements. Grand Rapids, MI: Regency Reference Library, 1988 Published by Zondervans.
[8] Ibid
[5] Ibid
[9] "The History of Our Women's Organization," from a souvenir book, New York, May 7-11, 1952. Page 33-34
[8] Ibid
[10] Moore, Joanna P. Christian Hope Magazine. "History of the Bible Band by Mother Lizzie Robinson". Printed in April, 1937.
[9] Ibid
[9] Ibid
[5] Ibid
[9] Ibid
[5] Ibid
[11] The Year Book of the Church of God in Christ for the Year 1926. Compiled by Lillian Brooks Coffey. "Mother Robinson's Report---1925". Pages 77-78.
[8] Ibid
[9] Ibid

[25] Patterns on the Landscape Heritage Conservation in North Omaha. Report prepared by Omaha City Planning Department & The Landmarks Heritage Preservation Commission. Published by Klopp Printing Company, Omaha, Nebraska, 1984.

[12] Omaha City Directory Co's City Directory of Greater Omaha. Omaha, NE: Omaha Directory Co., 1911-1914, 1916-1918.
[12] Ibid
[10] Ibid
[10] Ibid
[13] Department of Public Relations Church of God in Christ, comp. Church of God in Christ the Hour Glass Report: Reflections of Past and Present. Memphis, Tenn. Pages 24-25.
[7] Ibid
[7] Ibid
[11] Ibid
[7] Ibid
[7] Ibid
[7] Ibid
[9] Ibid
[7] Ibid
[7] Ibid
[14] 64th Annual Holy Convocation of the Church of God in Christ Western Missouri Jurisdiction. Printed in August 1980. "Autobiography Bishop Virgil Moses Barker—1880-1974". Pg. 5.
[14] Ibid
[14] Ibid
[5] Ibid
[8] Ibid
[8] Ibid
[5] Ibid
[8] Ibid
[9] Ibid
[15] Women's International Convention May 1956. Published by D.J. Young Publishing House. "The Beginning History of the Women's Work". 1956, Page 8.

[16] Landmarks Case File H1-92-4. "Minutes Public Hearing and Administrative Meeting Landmarks Heritage Preservation Commission…." Omaha, NE, 12 February 1992.
[16] Mount Hope Cemetery, Omaha, Nebraska. Lot and Plate Historic Records. 1920.
[11] Ibid
[12] Ibid
[17] The Women's International Conventions Souvenir. "Memorial Tribute Elect Lady Robinson" 1957, printed. Page 9.
[18] County Clerk, Douglas County, NE: "Articles of Incorporation of Church of God in Christ of Omaha, Nebraska"; August 3, 1925.
[18] Ibid
[11] Ibid
[11] Ibid
[5] Ibid
[11] Ibid
[11] Ibid
[19] Rules of the Women's Work of the Church of God in Christ. By Mother Lizzie Robinson. Adopted 15th Annual Setting of the Women's Work. December 15, 1926, Memphis, Tenn.

[9]Ibid
[7] Ibid
[24] Glimpses into the life of a great Mississippian and a majestic American Educator 1926-1976. By E. M. Lashley. Published in Brooklyn, New York 1977.
[24] Ibid
[7] Ibid
[7] Ibid
[7] Ibid
[20] Omaha World Herald. Death Certificates, evening edition, 2 March 1937; Obituaries, evening edition, 18 December 1945.
[13] Ibid
[21] Facts About the Temple Dedication Booklet. "Personal Letter Written by Mother Lizzie Robinson". By Bishop R.F. Williams and Elder U.E. Miller. Printed 1945. Page 35.

[22] McCord, Julia. "Bishop Urges Church of God in Christ to Return to Roots." Omaha World-Herald. 21 September 1991, 65-66.